# Kate Fortune's Journal Entry

*Can the Fortune family get together without some misadventure always happening? Judging by the latest fiasco in which my Isabelle ran away from her own wedding, I suspect not. Still, I can't help but be relieved that Isabelle finally saw the light and acted with some gumption. In spite of what her parents said, she had no business marrying that Brad Rowan. Even I could see that he wasn't on the up and up.*

*According to the Fortune rumor mill, the investigator hired to look into Mike Dodd's murder is now protecting her from Brad at a secluded mountain cabin. I've already seen how Isabelle and Link look at each other. And I can't stop hoping that Isabelle will own up to her feelings and put this poor man out of his misery...by marrying him!*

Dear Reader,

The year 2000 has been a special time for Silhouette, as we've celebrated our 20th anniversary. Readers from all over the world have written to tell us what they love about our books, and we'd like to share with you part of a letter from Carolyn Dann of Grand Bend, Ontario, who's a fan of Silhouette Desire. Carolyn wrote, "I like the storylines…the characters…the front covers… All the characters in the books are the kind of people you like to read about. They're all down-to-earth, everyday people." And as a grand finale to our anniversary year, Silhouette Desire offers six of your favorite authors for an especially memorable month's worth of passionate, powerful, provocative reading!

We begin the lineup with the always wonderful Barbara Boswell's MAN OF THE MONTH, *Irresistible You,* in which a single woman nine months pregnant meets her perfect hero while on jury duty. The incomparable Cait London continues her exciting miniseries FREEDOM VALLEY with *Slow Fever.* Against a beautiful Montana backdrop, the oldest Bennett sister is courted by a man who spurned her in their teenage years. And *A Season for Love,* in which Sheriff Jericho Rivers regains his lost love, continues the new miniseries MEN OF BELLE TERRE by beloved author BJ James.

Don't miss the thrilling conclusion to the Desire miniseries FORTUNE'S CHILDREN: THE GROOMS in Peggy Moreland's *Groom of Fortune.* Elizabeth Bevarly will delight you with *Monahan's Gamble.* And *Expecting the Boss's Baby* is the launch title of Leanne Banks's new miniseries, MILLION DOLLAR MEN, which offers wealthy, philanthropic bachelors guaranteed to seduce you.

We hope all readers of Silhouette Desire will treasure the gift of this special month.

Happy holidays!

*Joan Marlow Golan*

Joan Marlow Golan
Senior Editor, Silhouette Desire

Please address questions and book requests to:
Silhouette Reader Service
U.S.: 3010 Walden Ave., P.O. Box 1325, Buffalo, NY 14269
Canadian: P.O. Box 609, Fort Erie, Ont. L2A 5X3

# Groom of Fortune
## PEGGY MORELAND

Published by Silhouette Books
**America's Publisher of Contemporary Romance**

Special thanks and acknowledgment are given
to Peggy Moreland for her contribution
to the Fortune's Children: The Grooms series.

To Leanne Banks, Kathryn Jensen, Shawna Delacorte and
Caroline Cross. It was an honor to participate with you all in this
series and a thrill to add another limb to the Fortune family tree.

 SILHOUETTE BOOKS

ISBN 0-373-76336-0

GROOM OF FORTUNE

Copyright © 2000 by Harlequin Books S.A.

Visit Silhouette at www.eHarlequin.com

**Printed in U.S.A.**

## PEGGY MORELAND

published her first romance with Silhouette in 1989 and continues to delight readers with stories set in her home state of Texas. Winner of the National Readers' Choice Award, a nominee for the *Romantic Times Magazine* Reviewer's Choice Award and a finalist for the prestigious RITA Award, Peggy has appeared on the *USA Today* and Waldenbooks bestseller lists. When not writing, she enjoys spending time at the farm riding her quarter horse, Lo-Jump. She, her husband and three children make their home in Round Rock, Texas. You may write to Peggy at P.O. Box 2453, Round Rock, TX 78680-2453.

# FORTUNE'S Children

*Meet the Arizona Fortunes—a family with a legacy of wealth, influence and power. As they gather for a host of weddings, a shocking plot against the family is revealed...and passionate new romances are ignited.*

**ISABELLE FORTUNE:** She'd narrowly escaped marrying a murderer. But now, stranded alone in a remote cabin with Link Templeton, her heart was facing an even greater danger!

**LINK TEMPLETON:** This streetwise man had pulled himself up from the gutter by his bootstraps, but now he was facing his biggest challenge—staying away from a woman thirteen years his junior, a woman whose innocence and privileged background posed a stark contrast to his own. A woman he'd lusted after for nearly a year.

**BRAD ROWAN:** He'd offered Isabelle Fortune a marriage deal he *thought* she couldn't refuse, but now she suspected him of murder!

# One

She didn't love him.

She wasn't sure she even liked him.

Yet, within minutes she would become his wife.

Having slipped away unnoticed by her attendants, Isabelle Fortune stood in the vestibule with her fingers clutched tightly around her bridal bouquet, her nose pressed against the sanctuary door's tiny window, watching her fiancé enter the sanctuary through the side door and walk toward the altar. Dressed in black tails and wearing a confident smile, Brad Rowan looked very much the part of the eager groom.

And Isabelle felt like a lamb being led to slaughter.

With a shudder, she forced her gaze away from Brad and to the pews already crowded with family and friends. More than a thousand engraved wedding invitations had been mailed, and it appeared that not a one of the recipients had sent their regrets. Not that she was surprised. When the Fortunes threw a party, no matter what the occasion, all of Pueblo turned out for the event, knowing that the Fortunes would spare no expense.

And they wouldn't be disappointed this time, either. The caterers her parents had hired had worked frantically for days, preparing the succulent hors d'oeuvres, entrées and desserts for the wedding reception, while a crew of workers readied the grounds of the Fortune estate for the outdoor gala, already touted as the social event of the year. A new marble fountain flown in from Italy had been installed in the swimming pool, and the gardens had been pruned and filled with a colorful array of flowering plants. White canvas canopies dotted the sprawling lawn, and a portable dance floor and a stage for the orchestra had been constructed beneath the largest of the tents.

No, the Fortunes had spared no expense in marrying off their only daughter.

A knot of dread formed in Isabelle's stomach as she slowly scanned the ornately decorated church illuminated by hundreds of flickering candles, a glimmering reminder of the money invested in this day. Tall, slender tapers stood on the ledges of the windows, bringing to life the scenes depicted on the etched stained glass. Behind the altar, a dozen gracefully curved silver candelabra pedestals held even more of the slender tapers, while towering, fat columns of wax rose from the ropes of ivy on the altar's railing.

Mesmerized by the flickering candles, she stared,

the dread twisting tighter and tighter, until Brad stepped into her line of vision again, making her flinch. She watched him stop in front of the altar and take his place to the right of the priest, her fingers convulsing on the ribbon-wrapped stem of her bouquet. She knew it was considered bad luck for a bride to see her groom on the day of their wedding, but considering the fact that her marriage was a mockery, devoid of any emotion other than that of duty, she didn't think that luck, good or bad, would have much effect on the success of their union.

Regret over her hasty decision to accept Brad's marriage proposal burned through her, momentarily overriding the dread, and she was helpless to force it back. She was sacrificing her life, her dreams, for her parents, a payback of sorts for all they'd suffered and sacrificed for her through the years.

And she wondered now if it wasn't all a colossal mistake, one that she'd regret for the rest of her life.

If she had any courage at all, she fretted, she'd leave right now, before the ceremony began. And why not? she thought, grasping at the idea. She'd simply tell her parents she couldn't go through with the marriage, that she didn't love Brad, that she'd only accepted his proposal for their sakes, so that the Fortune family could claim ownership to Lightfoot's Plateau, and preserve the cave used as a spiritual retreat by Native American tribes, restoring it in memory of their ancestor, Natasha Lightfoot, Isabelle's grandmother.

She'd explain it all to them, she told herself, relief flooding through her. They'd understand.

But the relief was short-lived as her gaze strayed to the candelabra and the candles that flickered there. She caught her lower lip between her teeth, reminded of her parents' delight in her marriage to Brad. Would they understand? she wondered, doubt niggling at her confidence. Or would they...

She jumped at a sound that came from behind her, and spun to see the entry door swinging open. Not wanting to be seen, she looked wildly around for a place to hide. Grabbing fistfuls of satin, she gathered up the skirt of her wedding gown and ran, ducking quickly behind the partially open door of the coat closet. Holding her breath, she listened to the echo of footsteps on the vestibule's marble floor.

"Are we late?" came a man's low voice.

"I don't think so" was the reply, "though the music's already started."

"Lucky son of a bitch," she heard the first man mutter. "Marrying into all that money."

Her mouth gaping, Isabelle leaned closer to the partially open door, straining to hear. The voice sounded vaguely familiar, but she couldn't put a face to it.

There was a wry laugh from the other man. "As if he didn't already have a direct pipeline into the Fortune's bank account."

The first man laughed, too. "The greedy son of a bitch."

"Greedy, hell. He's a genius, and we're damn lucky to be in on the take."

"Yeah," the first agreed. "Though I have to admit I was worried there for a bit when Mike started demanding a bigger slice of the pie."

*Mike?* Isabelle repeated silently in confusion. *Mike Dodd?* Though she hadn't personally known the construction foreman who had been killed earlier that year in an elevator crash at the site of the Children's Hospital her family was building, she had been affected by his death, as had all the Fortune family. But what pie were the men talking about? She pressed her ear closer to the door, hoping to hear more.

"Brad handled it," the second man was saying. "That guy's cool as a cucumber when under pressure. Cold-blooded, he is, and that's a fact."

Isabelle pressed a hand against her mouth to stifle the startled cry that rose. Her fiancé was involved in Mike Dodd's death? But how? Why?

"Easy enough when there's nothing but ice running in your veins."

Numbed by what she'd overheard, Isabelle listened as the sanctuary door squeaked open on its hinges. Organ music spilled out into the church's vestibule as the latecomers slipped inside the nave. Then, only silence.

Isabelle sagged weakly against the coat closet's door, her eyes wide, her hand still clamped over her mouth.

Oh, God. If what she'd overheard was true, then her fiancé was responsible for Mike Dodd's death.

And within minutes, she would become the wife of a murderer.

Link Templeton glanced at the clock on his dash, then back at the street ahead, and pressed the accelerator a little closer to the floor. He had to get to the

church before it was too late. He had to get there
before the wedding took place.

He downshifted to third, made the turn onto
Feather Road on two wheels, then stomped down on
the accelerator again, fishtailing for a moment before
he was able to bring the city-issue, four-wheel-drive
Blazer under control. Perspiration beaded his forehead
and ran in an irritating trickle between his shoulder
blades.

He knew in his gut that Brad Rowan was guilty of
murder. Though he had no sound evidence to back
up his theory, other than the papers found by Mike
Dodd's sister, Angelica, and given to Link by Angelica's lawyer, Cynthia Fortune, which pointed to a
deliberate cover-up. And he'd learned over the years
to trust his gut instincts on a case. They were rarely
wrong.

The papers *had* provided him with the information
he needed to clear Riley Fortune as a suspect in the
murder case though, and they had substantiated
Link's theory that Brad was the man responsible for
Dodd's murder. But Link still lacked the solid evidence he needed to put Rowan behind bars and win
a conviction in a trial.

Evidence or not, he told himself, he had to stop the
wedding before it was too late.

But how would Isabelle take the news when he told
her that the man she loved was a murderer?

She'd hate him. He'd had enough experience handing out bad news in his job as a criminal investigator
for the city of Pueblo to know that the messenger
rarely received any praise from the family and friends

of the accused. Hadn't he already felt the sting of the Fortunes' outrage when he'd been forced to arrest Riley Fortune, Isabelle's brother, as a suspect in the death of Mike Dodd?

He growled low in his throat, glaring at the road ahead. It didn't matter what Isabelle Fortune *or* her family thought of him. It was the case that was important. It was slapping iron on a guilty man's wrists and jerking another criminal off the streets that brought him satisfaction. It was his job.

But stopping a society wedding wasn't.

He slapped an angry palm against the steering wheel. But he couldn't just stand by and permit Isabelle to marry Brad Rowan. Not when he knew the man was capable of murder. What if, after their marriage, Isabelle happened upon some bit of information that pointed to Brad's guilt? Would Brad kill her, too, as he had Mike Dodd, to silence her? The very thought had Link curling his fingers tighter around the steering wheel. He wouldn't let Brad harm her. He couldn't. He—

He shoved the unwanted thoughts away, but try as he might, he couldn't erase the image of Isabelle the thoughts had drawn. He remembered the day when he'd dropped by Cynthia Fortune's and had stumbled, unknowingly, into a wedding shower held in Isabelle's honor. When his gaze had met Isabelle's across the room, it was as if lightning had struck. He'd stood immobile, paralyzed by the violet eyes that met his, his pulse pounding in his ears, every nerve in his body burning with awareness.

And he was sure that she'd been similarly affected.

A laugh from a guest was what had finally shocked him into movement. He'd torn his gaze from hers and turned away...but he'd never forgotten the look in her eyes. The awareness. The desire. He'd recognized them, because he'd lived with both ever since that day.

He snorted in disgust. She's in love with another man, he reminded himself. And even if she wasn't, he was too old and too jaded to make a play for a woman like her.

He caught a flash of red in the church parking lot ahead, then a convertible sports car shot out of the lot and directly into his path. "Damn!" He stomped on the brake, whipping the steering wheel to the right to avoid broadsiding the small foreign car.

His heart pumping like a jackhammer, he stared after the car, watching as the woman behind the wheel ripped a wedding veil from her head and held it up, letting the wind have it. The delicate lace panels sailed behind her for a moment, then floated slowly to the street, like a kite with a broken string.

Isabelle? he asked himself, recognizing the pricey foreign car and its driver. Where was she going? She was supposed to be getting married. What the hell had happened?

He glanced toward the church for an answer, but the thick entry doors were closed. And though the parking lot was full, there wasn't a soul in sight. He glanced again in the direction of the red sports car, then back to the church where the wedding was to have taken place. *It's none of your business,* he told himself. *You've got no jurisdiction when it comes to Isabelle Fortune's personal affairs.*

"Like hell, I don't," he muttered. Setting his jaw, he turned his face to the street ahead, stomped on the clutch and shifted into first. Peeling out and leaving a trail of black rubber in his wake, he took off in the direction the red sports car had taken.

Isabelle fairly flew along the stretch of two-lane highway that led into the desert, intent on nothing but putting miles between her and the church. She drove for nearly an hour, her mind frozen, her fingers cinched tightly around the wheel. The wind whipped tendrils loose from her upswept hair and stung her eyes, but she was oblivious to everything but the white line that stretched in front of her.

A raindrop splattered against the windshield. Another struck her cheek, a needle-sharp pain, jolting her from her trancelike state. Glancing up, she saw that the sky had turned an ominous yellowish-green. She slowed, guiding her car to the shoulder. With fingers that shook uncontrollably, she pressed the electronic switch to raise the convertible's top, locked it into place, then accelerated back onto the highway.

She didn't know where she was going. But her destination wasn't important. The only thing that mattered was getting away.

Tears filled her eyes. What would her parents say when they discovered her missing? Would they be angry? Worried? What would all the guests say when they realized the bride had run away and left the groom at the altar?

*Brad.*

What would he say? Do? Would he follow her?

*Murderer.*

A shiver chased down her spine at the reminder.

It was so hard to believe, yet something deep inside her told her it was true. Although she'd known Brad most of her life, she'd never completely trusted him. Granted, he'd never been anything but polite and attentive to her, especially since their engagement three months ago, but she'd always felt as if a different personality lurked beneath his carefully groomed facade.

She shivered again as the rain fell harder, hammering her car and obstructing her view of the road ahead. She switched on the windshield wipers and tightened her hands on the wheel. Storms came up quickly in the desert and could be treacherous, she knew.

And Isabelle had never liked storms, a fact her brothers had often teased her about.

She bit back a scream when a clap of thunder, so loud it nearly deafened her, shook her low-slung car. It was followed by a flash of lightning that ripped like a knife across the almost black sky, seemingly splitting it in two.

Wishing that she'd chosen another direction in which to run, Isabelle glanced frantically around, looking for somewhere safe to wait out the storm… but there was nothing but miles of desert surrounding her and the shadowed hump of dark mountains ahead.

She drove on, the rain continuing to batter her car,

her emotions, shattering her already frayed nerves. Lightning flashed dangerously close to the earth time and time again in front of her. Thunder crashed violently around her, until the sound echoed continuously in her head, winding her nerves tighter and tighter.

Hoping to find a radio station with a weather report or, at the very least, some soothing music to block out the sounds of the storm, she reached for the control panel. At the same moment, the car's front tires hit a sheet of water on the highway and the steering wheel was wrenched from her hand. She bit back a scream as she grabbed for the wheel, gripping it with both hands, trying to regain control. But the car spun crazily, around and around and around, then slammed into the ditch.

A scream rent the air. Her own.

Darkness followed.

Link hung back, not wanting Isabelle to know he was following her. He feared that if she picked up on the tail, she might panic and end up wrecking her car. And at the speed she was traveling, he was pretty sure she wouldn't walk away from the accident unharmed.

When the rain started, he shortened the distance between them, but stayed only close enough to keep her taillights in sight.

"Slow down, Isabelle," he warned under his breath.

He'd no sooner muttered the warning when a bolt of lightning lit up the sky, illuminating her car fully. He saw the water that covered the low spot in the highway ahead and prayed she saw it, too. Pressing the accelerator closer to the floor, he closed the distance between them, silently willing her to slow down.

"Oh, God, no," he moaned when he realized the sports car was out of control. He eased on the brake, his heart lurching to his throat while he watched helplessly as the car in front of him spun wildly, headed straight for the ditch. Whipping the steering wheel of his Blazer to the right, he slid to a stop on the shoulder of the highway, jerked on the emergency brake and jumped out. Rain stung his face, blinding him as he ran for her car. Within seconds he was drenched to the skin.

He jerked open the door on the driver's side but could see only the top of her head above the inflated air bag. "Isabelle!" he yelled, trying to make himself heard over the pounding rain. When she didn't respond, he rammed his hand into his jeans pocket in search of his knife.

"Isabelle!" he shouted again, louder. "Hang on. I'll get you out." He stabbed his knife into the air bag, ripping a long slit to speed its deflation, then pressed both hands against it, forcing out the air. Shoving the bag out of his way, he bent over her. Her face was covered with the fine white powder the air bag had emitted. Carefully, he brushed it away, searching her face for any sign of injury, then moved his fingers to the long, smooth column of her throat, feeling for a pulse. Relieved to find one, though thready, he hunkered down beside her and framed her face with his hands. "Isabelle," he whispered, frightened by the paleness of her skin, eyes that remained stubbornly closed.

After what seemed an eternity, her eyelashes fluttered and her lids slowly lifted. He could see that her pupils were dilated, and was sure that, although conscious, she wasn't aware of his presence. He grabbed her hands and chafed them between his own. "You're all right," he told her, as if in saying it, he could make it true. "You're going to be okay now."

She blinked twice, slowly bringing him into focus. "Link?" she whispered in disbelief.

"Yeah, it's me. I followed you from the church."

Tears flooded her violet eyes. "Oh, Link," she cried, and fell against his chest.

He wrapped his arms around her and shifted his weight until he was sitting on the edge of the seat beside her. "It's okay," he murmured, stroking a hand over her wind-tangled raven-black hair. "I've got you. You're all right now."

She tightened her arms around his neck, holding on as if her very life depended on it. "You've got to help me," she sobbed hysterically. "I've got to get away."

"Shh," he soothed. "Don't worry. I'll take care of you."

Rain streamed down his back, reminding him of the storm and his need to get them to safety. He pushed her to arm's length. "Are you hurt?"

Her breath hitched, and she lifted her gaze to his, her wide eyes drenched and darkened with fear. "N-no, I d-don't think so." She pressed her palm between her breasts. "Just m-my chest."

He slid from the seat to stand outside the car, then leaned back inside, his face inches from hers in the cramped quarters. "I'm going to carry you to my truck. If you feel any pain, tell me."

Her breath hitched again, and she nodded, never once moving her gaze from his. "All right."

"Here," he said, and took her arm and guided it around his neck. "Hold on to me." He slipped one hand beneath her knees and the other behind her back. "Ready?"

"Y-yes," she stammered, her teeth beginning to chatter.

Straightening, he lifted her from the car, then looked down at her. Rain sluiced down his face and over his chin, dropping to stain the satin of her wedding gown. Bowing his head over hers and hunching his shoulders, he tried his best to protect her from the worst of the storm's fury. "You okay?" he asked, raising his voice to be heard over the storm that continued to rage around them. "Any pain?"

"I'm o-okay." She tucked her face into the curve of his neck. "P-please. Just h-hurry."

He jogged his way back to his truck, slipping and sliding on the rain-slick ground. When he reached his truck, he braced her against the side in order to free a hand to open the door. Quickly, he slid her onto the seat, then straightened, his breath coming in hard, grabbing gasps. "I'll be right back. I need to lock up your car."

He slammed the door and ran back for her vehicle. He ducked inside and grabbed the keys from the ignition. As he withdrew, he noticed the suitcase on the back seat and grabbed it, too. By the time he reached the Blazer again, his boots were saturated with water and felt as if they were filled with cement. He heaved her suitcase into the back, then hopped inside the truck, slamming the door behind him. He dragged a hand down his face, wiping away the rain, then braced a hand against the steering wheel and turned to face her. Her gaze was on his, her eyes wide, her lips trembling. Her fingers were twisted into a knot on her lap. "You okay?"

She nodded. "Y-yes. Th-thank you."

Always polite. Always the lady. But there was an edge of desperation, of hysteria, behind the polite manners. "What happened?"

"I—I lost c-control of my c-car."

"I mean before. At the church."

"I—I ran away."

He watched her eyes fill again, and hated himself for asking. But he had to know. "Last-minute jitters?"

The violet eyes turned stormy, wild, and she grabbed for him, her nails biting deeply into his forearm. "I've got to get away. Please, Link," she begged. "You've got to help me."

Seeing the panic swirling in her eyes and hearing the hysteria rising in her voice, he knew he couldn't press her for answers. Not now. He stared at her a moment, wondering if he'd regret asking the one question he needed answered. "Do you trust me?"

When she hesitated a second too long, he looked away, scowling at the rain-streaked windshield and the shadowed mountains ahead. "Doesn't matter," he said gruffly, and reached for the ignition key. ''Right now I'm your only hope.''

The decision to head for the mountains with Isabelle wasn't one Link made easily...nor was the drive he made to reach them. The storm that had blown up so quickly in the desert decided to hang around awhile, seemingly chasing them into the mountains and making the narrow roads treacherous to navigate in the growing darkness. More than once Link had felt the Blazer's tires spin on the muddy incline and the rear of the vehicle fishtail out of control. Even with the four-wheel drive engaged, progress up the mountain was slow and tedious.

By the time he reached the well-concealed turnoff he'd been watching for, the tendons in his neck and shoulders felt like steel rods and a headache was punching him between his eyes. After making the turn, he glanced over at Isabelle and found her still curled against the passenger door asleep. How she'd been able to sleep through the hair-raising drive, he wasn't sure. But after assuring himself she hadn't suffered a head injury, he had let her sleep, thankful that she could. He wasn't in the mood to make polite conversation...not that he'd know how.

*She* was the one with the manners, he reminded himself bitterly. All those years spent at that fancy boarding school back east where her parents had sent her, the finishing school in Europe that followed. The only school Link's parents had ever sent him to was the school of hard knocks.

He bit back a growl and turned his face away from

her, narrowing an eye at the road ahead and the trees that crowded it on both sides. But it was that school of hard knocks that had nudged him toward law enforcement, he reminded himself, and it was that same school that had given him the instincts he needed to succeed where others had failed.

And those instincts were the ones he'd use to protect Isabelle. Keep her alive.

The Blazer's headlights bounced off the cabin's windows and reflected the light back at the Blazer, making Link squint. He slowed, downshifting as he pulled as close to the front porch as he dared. Switching off the engine, he turned to look at Isabelle again. Asleep she looked even more innocent and fragile than she did when she was awake…and, if possible, more beautiful. He reached out a hand to brush the tendril of hair that curled like a damp question mark against her cheek…but caught himself just shy of touching her. That porcelain skin. All that womanliness. That innocence. Curling his fingers into a fist, he withdrew his hand and turned to shoulder open his door.

The storm had lost most of its steam and now only a light rain fell, misting his face and hair as he circled to the passenger side of the truck. He opened the door carefully, not wanting to startle her. "Isabelle?" he said softly. When she didn't respond, he leaned inside, bracing one hand against the dashboard and laying the other on her shoulder. "Isabelle," he said, gently shaking her. "Wake up. We're here."

She moaned softly and turned away, snuggling her cheek deeper against the Blazer's worn upholstery.

With a glance over his shoulder at the dilapidated cabin he was taking her to, he decided it might be better to let her sleep. He guided her arm around his neck and scooped her up into his arms, then headed for the porch. As he brushed past the post that supported the sagging front porch, the train of her dress snagged on the rough cedar, stopping him. He gave the train a sharp tug and swore under his breath when he heard the delicate fabric rip.

She awoke then, shoving at his chest as she tried to struggle free.

He tightened his grip on her. "Be still now, or you're going to make me drop you."

Her fingers froze on his neck as her eyes snapped to his. He saw the remembrance slowly settle there… as well as the fear.

She tore her gaze from his and glanced nervously around. "Wh-where are we?"

"At a buddy of mine's cabin in the mountains. You'll be safe here," he added as she turned those wide, violet eyes on his again.

"He can't find me," she whispered, her grip on him growing desperate. "Please don't let him find me."

Something twisted in Link's gut as he looked down at her. Something he thought he'd lost long ago. The ability to care. "He won't find you," he said gruffly, and reached for the door. "Not on this mountain. Nobody could."

He pushed open the door and caught up her train as he hefted her higher in his arms. As he stepped inside the cabin, he was struck at the irony in that gesture. Link Templeton carrying a bride across a threshold. The man who'd sworn he'd never marry, who'd sworn he'd never be foolish enough to fall in love, was carrying a bride across a threshold.

The only comfort he found in that thought was that the bride wasn't his.

She was a runaway.

# Two

After stripping off his wet shirt and changing into a pair of dry jeans he found in the closet, bare-chested Link pulled fresh linens from the dresser drawer and began making the bed. Anxious to finish the job before Isabelle emerged from the bathroom, he kept an ear cocked to the sounds coming from behind the door she'd closed between them. The soft gurgle of water as it ran from the ancient faucet and splashed into the rust-stained sink. The dull thump of a satin heel striking the old footed tub, or perhaps the side of the toilet. The whisper of satin and lace as it whisked against the scarred plank floor.

He tried not to think about Isabelle unbuttoning that long row of tiny, satin-covered buttons, of slipping the dress from her shoulders and letting it fall to the floor. Of her stepping from the cloud of white, her bare flesh pebbling as the cabin's cool air struck it…the bobbing of ripe, full breasts, free now from constraints…the feminine curve of her waist…the heart-shaped buttocks he'd already defined earlier when he'd carried her into the cabin.

But the vision was there, filling his mind and making his fingers knot in the quilt he held.

Furious with himself and his wayward thoughts, he sailed the quilt over the freshly made bed, then stretched to tuck one end under the foot of the mattress. He jerked his head up when the hinges on the bathroom door squeaked. His breath locked in his lungs as Isabelle stepped into the opening, dressed in an ankle-length gown and robe of ivory silk. She looked as virginal and nervous as any bride might on her wedding night. Straightening slowly, he let the quilt slip from slack fingers and simply stared, letting his gaze slide from liquid eyes to bare toes that curled self-consciously against the hardwood floor.

Her hair hung past her shoulders, its dark ends curling gently around the swell of each breast, emphasizing their fullness and the twin knots of flesh puckered at their peaks. The silk hugged her body like a second skin, skimming over her flat abdomen, molding her slim hips, rising above the sharp planes of her pelvic bones, then dipping slightly into the juncture of her legs, before tumbling like a moonlit waterfall to her feet. When his gaze reached the gown's hem, he saw the fabric's slight quivering and realized it was caused by trembling knees.

Slowly, he moved his gaze back to her face. "My

God'' was all he could say when his eyes met hers again.

Color flamed in her already flushed cheeks and she hugged one arm at her waist while crossing the other over her breasts. She pressed her fingertips at her throat in a failed attempt to cover herself. "I—I'm sorry," she said, dropping her gaze from his. "All I have with me is my trousseau, the clothes I packed for my honeymoon."

Link forced a swallow, then drew in a ragged breath. "No problem," he murmured, his voice sounding raw even to his own ears. But it was a problem, he knew. A big one. There was no way he'd be able to stay in the cabin with her. Not with her dressed like that. Not and keep his hands off her.

But he had no other choice.

Knowing that, he scowled as he strode to the closet, snatched a flannel shirt from a hanger and tossed it to her. "Put this on," he ordered gruffly, then pulled another out and shrugged it on to cover his own bare chest. "I found a can of stew in the pantry," he said, and gestured toward the bedroom doorway and the main room beyond, indicating for her to precede him. "It's probably hot by now."

With an uneasy glance his way, Isabelle darted for the door. Link watched her and slowly released the breath he'd held. How he'd ever survive the night without touching her, he didn't know.

But it was his duty to keep her safe, he reminded himself. And Link Templeton was a man who honored duty above all else. Even his own safety.

His own sanity.

Setting his jaw, he followed her into the kitchen, pulled down heavy mugs from the cupboard and filled them with the thick stew while she hung back, watching, her arms hugging the flannel shirt over her breasts. He gestured with one of the mugs toward the small, crude table, waited until she was seated, then plunked a mug down in front of her and sat down in the chair opposite hers.

Picking up a spoon, he stirred, keeping his gaze on his stew, watching the steam rise from it. "Think you can tell me now what happened at the church?" he asked after a moment.

When she didn't immediately respond, he glanced up to find her gaze on his hands. Her eyes slid up to his. Their gazes met, held for a moment, his narrowing in steely determination, hers going from shy curiosity to fear in the time it took for his heart to take one more rib-threatening kick at the mere sight of her.

"I'm a cop," he said gruffly. "You have nothing to fear from me."

"You arrested my brother."

Link frowned at the accusation in her tone. "I had no choice. The evidence was there against him."

She fisted her hands on the tabletop and leaned toward him, her defensive stance taking him by surprise. A lamb turning lioness before his eyes. "Riley didn't kill Mike," she said angrily. "You know him better than that. Riley would never harm anyone."

Yes, Link acknowledged silently. In his gut, he had known that. In his heart, too, if he thought he had one. But gut instincts didn't hold any weight in a court of law. Evidence did. And the evidence stacked against Riley Fortune had been damning. So, Link had done his duty, arrested a man for a crime he knew he didn't commit...then busted his ass to uncover the evidence he needed to clear his name. Now all he needed was enough evidence to win a conviction against the real murderer. But Isabelle didn't know any of that, nor would he tell her.

"Do you know who did?" he asked instead.

He heard her quick inhalation of breath, saw her body stiffen, before she dropped her gaze to the hands she still held fisted on the table. "Yes," she said, her voice trembling. She slicked her tongue across lips that fear had parched. "I know who killed Mike."

"Who?" he asked, needing to hear her name the man his gut told him was responsible for the crime, the man the current evidence pointed to. The man she'd planned to marry. The man he despised for no other reason than Isabelle Fortune had agreed to marry him.

Slowly she lifted her face until her eyes met his again. "Brad," she whispered, then said more strongly. "Brad Rowan."

The certainty with which she named her fiancé, the venom behind the accusation, took Link by surprise. He'd expected her to defend him, to try to protect the man she loved. "You have proof?"

"No. But Brad killed Mike. I know he did."

With a snort, Link dropped his spoon into the mug and reared his chair back on two legs, eyeing her sardonically. "I know a lot of guilty men who are walking the streets, but without proof, that's exactly where they're going to stay. On the streets. The same as Brad Rowan will."

Her lips parted on a shocked gasp, her eyes shooting wide. "What! You aren't going to arrest him?"

He lifted a shoulder. "On what grounds? On the circumstantial evidence I currently have? On your unfounded accusation?"

She yanked her hands to her lap and glared at him across the width of the table. "It isn't unfounded. I heard two men talking in the vestibule."

He dropped his chair back to all four legs. "What two men?"

She waved away the question. "I don't know. Just two men I overheard talking—"

The diamond engagement ring she wore caught the light and shimmered, drawing Link's gaze to it. She stopped when she realized that he wasn't listening to her any longer, then followed his gaze to the hand she held aloft. She stared at the ring, as if unaware until that moment that she still wore it. Then, with a whimper, she twisted the ring off and hurled it across the room. It bounced off the far wall, then fell to the floor, rolling a few feet before coming to a stop at the edge of a braided rug spread on the floor before the dark fireplace. The diamond caught the light again, glimmered, seeming to wink at Link, as if teasing him with all it symbolized.

Arching a brow, he slowly shifted his gaze back to hers. "Feel better?"

She scrubbed her fingers over the spot where the ring had rested for the last several months, as if ridding her skin of something vile. "Yes," she said, her breath hitching. "Much."

He pursed his lips and gave his chin a jerk. "Good. Now, about those two men…"

She drew in a deep breath, placed her palms over the top of the table as if to steady herself, and then told Link what she'd overheard. When she'd finished, she leaned forward, her eyes unwavering in their conviction as they met Link's. "He killed him. Brad killed Mike. I know he did."

"Did you recognize the voices?"

She caught her lip between her teeth as she sank slowly back against her chair. "No," she said, shaking her head. "Though they were both familiar."

"How can you be sure?"

"Because they were!" she cried, her frustration returning with a vengeance. "I've heard the voices before. Where, I'm not sure. But I've heard them."

Link leaned across the table, convinced that the two unidentified men were the key he needed to put Brad Rowan behind bars where he belonged. And Isabelle held that key. "Think, Isabelle," he growled. "Think. Without a name, or a place, I have nothing to go on."

Her eyes filled with tears and she pressed her fingers against her temples, shaking her head. "I've tried," she cried miserably. "While I was driving through the desert, their voices played through my mind over and over again, but I simply can't place them."

"Could they be friends of your father's? Employees of his?"

Her eyes flipped wide and she jumped to her feet,

knocking over her chair. "Oh, my God! My parents! They must be worried sick. I've got to call them." She whirled, searching for a phone, but Link lunged across the table, caught her by the arm and jerked her back around.

"You can't call your parents, Isabelle."

"Wh-what?" she stammered, blinking at him.

"No calls."

"But I have to!" She tugged her arm, trying to pull free. "They'll be worried. Frightened. I *have* to call them. I have to let them know where I am, that I'm all right."

Link rose and ducked a hip around the edge of the table, rounding it. He caught her other arm and forced her to face him. "Isabelle," he said, giving her a hard shake when she continued to struggle against him. "Listen to me. You can't call your parents. The call could be traced."

She stilled, her eyes going wide. "Traced?"

"Yes. Brad, or anyone else who wanted to, could trace the call to this cabin."

She shook her head, tears filling her eyes. "But my parents. They'll be sick with worry. You don't understand," she cried, and tried to pull free. "I was kidnapped when I was young. I know what they went through then. How much they suffered. I can't put them through that again. I just can't!"

Link scowled as he held on to her, refusing to let her go. He understood, all right. He knew all about the kidnapping of Isabelle Fortune. The memory of her parents' faces on the evening news when they'd offered a staggering reward for any information that would lead to the recovery of their daughter would forever be burned on his mind—as would the image of Isabelle's pale, haunted face when she'd been rescued three days later and returned safely to her parents.

He released her so quickly, she staggered back a step, unbalanced. "My cell," he said, and turned for the bedroom.

"What?" she said in confusion and hurried after him.

"My cell phone," he explained, pulling it from its holster on the belt of his wet jeans. He turned and held it out to her. "City issue. Calls can't be traced through it."

She reached for the phone, then glanced up at him in surprise when he didn't release his own grip on it.

"You can't tell them where you are," he warned, his blue eyes piercing hers. "Or that you're with me. If you do, you'll jeopardize your safety and that of your parents'. Do you understand?"

Frightened by the rigidity of his gaze and sobered by the threat he alluded to, she slowly nodded. "Y-yes. I understand."

He released the phone, and she turned away. She punched in her parents' number, then brought the phone to her ear. At the sound of her father's voice, she pressed her fingertips to her lips, forcing back tears. "Dad?"

"Isabelle," he cried in relief, making fresh tears flood her eyes. "My God, honey, where are you? Are you okay?" He clamped a hand over the mouthpiece and shouted for her mother, telling her that Isabelle was on the phone.

"Dad," she said loudly, trying to make herself heard over his shouting. "Please listen. I can't talk long. I just wanted you to know that I'm all right. That I'm safe."

Then her mother was on the phone, sobbing, "My baby, my baby. Isabelle, darling, where are you?"

"I'm okay, Mother," she said, struggling to keep the fear from her voice, the truth, not wanting to worry her parents any more than they already were. "I'm with—" She felt Link's hand clamp over hers and glanced up at him, saw the fierce, silent warning in his eyes. "I can't tell you where I am or who I'm with," she explained, her gaze frozen on Link's. "I just wanted you to know that I'm safe and that I'll be back in contact with you as soon as I can."

"Isabelle!" her mother wailed. "Darling, what is going on? Brad is beside himself with worry. He's in the library now. Your father's gone to tell him that you're on the phone."

Ice spilled through Isabelle's veins at the mention of her fiancé. "I can't talk to him," she said, her stomach knotting at the idea of him, a murderer, in her parents' home. "I have to go. I love you, Mother. Tell Dad that I love him, too." She quickly pressed the disconnect button, cutting off her mother's desperate pleas for her to remain on the line.

Link eased the phone from her paralyzed fingers and Isabelle turned away, covering her face with her hands. "Oh, God," she moaned. "They sounded so worried. So frightened. This must be just like it was before for them.''

She felt a hand on her shoulder, the gentle squeeze of comforting fingers through the flannel shirt. She turned and buried her face against his chest. ''I can't do this,'' she sobbed helplessly. ''I can't do this to them again. I've got to go home. Talk to them. Explain what's happened. Tell them about Brad.''

''No.'' When she twisted in his arms, trying to free herself from his embrace, Link tightened his arms around her. ''Isabelle,'' he ordered sternly, ''think what you're saying, what kind of danger you'd be placing yourself and your parents in. Brad's a murderer. You know that. You heard what those men said. Once Brad knows that you're aware of the part he played in Mike's death, he'll kill you, or try to, at the very least. He'll have to, in order to save his own hide.''

''But you didn't hear them, Link,'' she sobbed. ''They're so worried. It's just like before. I can't bear it,'' she cried, balling her hands against his chest. ''I can't put them through this again.''

''This isn't your fault,'' he told her, trying to calm her. ''And it wasn't your fault before, when you were kidnapped.''

''It is,'' she argued stubbornly. ''I shouldn't have run away. I should have stayed at the church, found my father and told him what I overheard.''

Furious that he couldn't make her understand the danger she was in, he pushed her to arm's length and gave her a hard shake. ''Don't you know what kind of man we're dealing with here? Brad Rowan's crazy.

Homicidal. If you'd stayed at the church and told your father what you overheard, Brad would have you by now, and God only knows what he would do to you to keep you quiet.'' He watched the blood drain from her face, saw the fear in her eyes and knew that he was frightening her even more than she already was. "Isabelle," he said, trying to keep his tone even, calm. "You did the right thing by running away. I can protect you here. I can keep you safe."

She stared up at him, wet violet eyes searching his. "Here?" she repeated. "We're staying here?"

"Yes."

"For how long?"

He set his jaw, wondering again how he'd survive being alone with her for even one night. "As long it takes to get the evidence I need to put Brad Rowan behind bars."

"But my parents…"

He released his hold on her. "As long as they are ignorant of Brad's guilt, he would have no reason to harm them."

"But—"

"I'll arrange for twenty-four hour surveillance for both them and Rowan. At the first sign of danger, I'll have Rowan arrested on suspicion of murder. Until then, I need for him to think his secret is safe, in hopes he'll make a mistake and lead us to the evidence we need to nail him."

Link dropped down onto the lumpy sofa with a weary sigh, scrubbed his hands over his face, then leaned forward, bracing his elbows on his thighs and his fists beneath his chin as he stared at the closed bedroom door.

Isabelle slept in the bed on the other side of the door. Isabelle Fortune. The woman he'd admired, even lusted after from afar, ever since her return to Pueblo less than a year earlier.

The irony of the situation didn't escape him.

Link Templeton, criminal investigator, lowly employee of the city that the Fortune family all but owned, hiding out in a remote cabin with the Fortune's only daughter, a woman thirteen years his junior, a woman whose innocence and privileged background was a stark contrast to the streetwise man who'd literally pulled himself from the gutter by his bootstraps.

As he stared at the door, knowing he was crazy for even thinking about her, an image of her as she'd appeared earlier that evening pushed itself, unwanted, into his mind. Standing in the bathroom doorway like a virginal bride on her wedding night. Her cheeks flushed, that thick mane of black hair framing a classically beautiful face and tumbling to hang past her slim shoulders. Breasts quivering beneath the thin silk that enhanced rather than concealed the feminine curves beneath it.

He could imagine himself stroking a hand down the smooth column of her throat, covering a breast, almost feel her flesh swell and arch against his palm, the heat rising from her skin to burn with his. Her head would drift back as he stroked her, her eyes would close, her lips part, and he would capture her mouth with his, sip at her sweetness, grow drunk on her erotic flavor, mate his tongue with hers even as he drew her hips hard against his.

Groaning at the image, he dived his fingers through his hair and held his head between his palms, trying to squeeze the lustful thoughts from his mind. "Crazy," he muttered under his breath. "Insane. Impossible. Irrational." Isabelle Fortune was out of his league, out of his realm. And *he* was out of his mind for even thinking about her. His job was to protect her. Nothing more.

Promising himself that he would remember that, he snatched his cell phone from the sofa beside him and quickly punched in a number.

"Hank," he said when his partner answered. "It's Link."

"Where the hell are you? Isabelle Fortune has disappeared, and the whole town is in an uproar. The chief wants you on the case."

"Isabelle's with me. We're at your cabin in the mountains."

"Whoa. Back up, buddy, and say that again."

Link sighed and dragged his palm over the top of his head, mussing his hair even more. "I've got Isabelle," he said again. "She's with me. I followed her when she left the church. She wrecked her car during the storm, and I picked her up and brought her to your cabin."

"Damn, Link. Brad Rowan is one angry groom. But his black mood doesn't come close to touching her old man's. Hunter Fortune's got the entire police force out looking for his daughter. He'll have your ass over a fire for this one, I can guaran-damn-tee it. You better get her back here, and fast.''

"No."

"No! Man, have you lost your mind? This is the Fortunes you're dealing with, and you're not exactly on their top-ten list since you arrested Riley and threw him in jail.''

"I know," Link said in frustration, "but I can't bring her back. She knows that Brad killed Mike Dodd.''

"The hell you say! Has she got proof?"

"No. That's the problem. Just prior to the wedding, she heard two men who alluded to Brad's involvement in Mike's murder, but she can't identify either one of them.''

"So you're going to keep her under wraps until she can?''

Link's scowl deepened. "It's the only way I know to keep her alive.'' He glanced at the door, then lowered his voice. "Listen. I need you to get me a list of all the wedding guests. I'm sure the Fortunes have a copy, but keep your reasons for needing it under your hat. I don't want them to know that Isabelle's with me, or that she suspects that Brad is the murderer.

"I need you to keep an eye on her parents," he continued, "as well as Rowan. If he shows any sign that he suspects Isabelle is aware of his guilt, arrest him and hold him on suspicion of murder until I can get there.''

"What about her car? Do you want me to have it towed in? A set of wheels like that? Somebody's bound to come along and strip it, and make a killing on the parts alone."

Link dragged a hand over his hair. "No. If you do, someone might suspect that you know something, know where she is. I'd rather her family suffer the financial loss of the car than have them face the emotional loss of their only daughter if Rowan should trace her back here to the cabin."

"Right."

"And cover for me, will you? Make up some story about me chasing down a lead in another city. Or, hell, tell 'em I quit. I don't care. Just don't let on that you know where I am or who's with me."

"My lips are sealed. And, buddy," Hank added, "watch your back. That Rowan is a cold son of a bitch and madder than a rabid dog. If he finds out you've got Isabelle..."

He let the warning drift off, unfinished. But Link didn't need to hear the warning to know the danger he had placed himself in. "Don't worry about me," he told Hank. "Just get me that guest list."

Isabelle awoke, screaming.

Link was awake and off the sofa and in the bedroom before she could fight her way free of the quilt tangled around her legs. He dropped down on the bed beside her and pulled her into his arms, trying to calm her.

She fought him like a wildcat, clawing at his chest and face with her hands and nails, while deafening him with bloodcurdling screams.

He wrapped his arms around her, successfully pinning her hands and arms between them. "Isabelle. Isabelle!" he shouted to be heard over her screams. "It's me. Link. I've got you. You're okay. Nobody's going to hurt you."

He repeated the same assurances over and over again until his voice, at last, penetrated the nightmare that seemed to hold her in its clutches. She grew still, though her body continued to tremble like a struck chord against his, her chest heaving against his with each grabbed breath. He drew her closer, his hands growing damp with the perspiration that soaked her gown and skin.

"It was just a dream," he told her, stroking a hand down her hair. "Just a dream."

She drew in a shuddery breath, another, then eased from his embrace and tipped her face up to his. In the darkness, her eyes were nothing but shadowed pools, her features indistinguishable. Needing to see her face, to reassure himself that she was all right, he stretched a hand behind him and switched on the bedside lamp. A soft golden glow spilled over the room, and when he turned back to her, he saw the wildness that flared in her eyes, the fear, and knew the nightmare still held her in its grip. "It was a dream," he told her again, and dragged a knuckle across her cheek, catching a stray tear. "Just a dream."

She shivered at his touch, her unblinking gaze locked on his. "Yes," she whispered, her voice hoarse from screaming. "A dream. A nightmare," she said on a low moan, and shivered again.

He wanted to draw her back into his arms, comfort her, but thought better of it. Instead, he shifted away, preparing to rise, to put some distance between them. "Are you okay now?"

She grabbed his arm before he could stand. "Please," she begged, her nails biting deep, her grip on him, as well as her gaze, desperate. "Don't leave me."

He sank back down beside her. "I won't," he promised. He slipped an arm around her shoulders, shifting her to his side, until their backs rested against the headboard. He stretched his legs out over the quilt still tangled with hers. "I'll stay with you as long as you want."

She seemed to wilt beneath his arm at his reassurance, her head dropping to rest on his shoulder. Her fingers found the edge of the quilt and drew it to her waist. "I'm sorry," she whispered, her voice breaking. "The nightmare. I don't have it often. Haven't in years." Her fingers curled into the fabric, her knuckles stark white against the colorful squares. "It's always the same. The men grabbing me, stuffing me into the back of the van."

A shiver shook her and he tightened his arm around her, held her firmly against his side. "The kidnapping?" he asked, though he was sure he knew her answer.

He felt her head move against his shoulder in silent assent.

"Yes," she whispered, her voice quivering with the horror of it. "The kidnapping. I was five. They took me to a cabin." She lifted her head from his shoulder to look uneasily around the room, slowly taking in her surroundings. The scarred chest of drawers. The dark windows with muslin drapes pushed back to let the dim moonlight filter through.

"Like this one," she said, as if just realizing the similarities. "But much more rustic. There was a bed," she added, and released her grip on the quilt to smooth a palm over the covers beside her hip. "Nothing more than a bare mattress, really, lying flat on the floor. No sheets. Just a dirty blanket. They kept me there for three days," she said, then turned her face up to his, her cheeks wet, her eyes haunted by the memory. "Three horrible, terrifying days."

He could only imagine the fear she must have felt if it was anything close to that which shadowed her eyes. Unable to bear thinking of what she might have suffered, seeing it reflected on her face, in her eyes, he lifted his hand and pressed his palm against her head, forcing it back down to his shoulder. "Don't think about it," he ordered, his voice husky. He turned his lips to her hair. "Block it from your mind."

He felt her stiffen, then she was shoving against his chest and from his embrace. "No," she said furiously, shocking him with the depth of her emotion. "Not any longer. I want to talk about it. All of it. But my family won't allow me. Every time I try, they change the subject or pretend they don't hear."

"It hurts them," he said, understanding all too well her family's avoidance of the subject. "Knowing how much you suffered, how terrified you were, hurts them. Hearing you speak of it would be forcing them to relive it again."

"But I *need* to talk about it," she cried. She

pressed her palms against the sides of her head. "The memories are here, in my mind, haunting me, and I need to let them out. To rid myself of them. But nobody will listen. They try to erase it all by pretending it never happened. They always have."

Her growing fury troubled him, as did her insistence to share the terrifying memories. He didn't want to hear the details of her kidnapping any more than her parents did, maybe less.

A teenager at the time of the incident, Link had followed the details of the kidnapping on television, along with the other citizens of Pueblo. But unlike the rest of Pueblo's citizens and the police force who were baffled by the few clues they had to follow, Link had exclusive information regarding Isabelle's kidnapping...information provided to him by his stepbrother, Joe Razley. Information the police weren't privy to.

But he'd listen to Isabelle recount the details of her kidnapping, he told himself, if only to ease her mind. "Tell me, then," he offered hesitantly.

She slicked her lips, inched closer, her gaze on his. "I ran away. Just like I did today."

He drew his head back frowning, sure that he'd known every detail of the kidnapping. But he'd never heard this one. "Ran away?"

"Yes," she said, obviously relieved to finally be able to tell it all. "I was angry with my parents because they wouldn't allow me to spend the night with one of my friends, so I decided to run away. I packed a backpack and snuck out of the house. I walked for miles, not really knowing where I planned to go, but determined to run away, to punish them.'' Tears filled her eyes and she dashed her fingertips across her cheeks, swiping them away.

"I made it all the way downtown,'' she said as the memories took her. "And I was frightened. More frightened than I'd ever been in my life. I never liked the dark. Always slept with a night-light on. There was a storm brewing. Much like the one today. Clouds covered the moon and stars and there was nothing but an occasional streetlight to relieve the shadows. I'd never walked alone in town, and I lost my way. I was crying, wanting to go back home, but unsure which way to go. A van pulled up to the curb beside me, and a man stuck his head out the window.'' She narrowed her eyes, as if, even now, she could picture his face in her mind. "He was young. Nineteen. Or maybe twenty. He had a scar at the corner of his eye.'' She touched her own face, demonstrating, then dropped her hand to her lap and gripped her fingers together.

"He asked me if I was lost. If I needed a ride. My parents had lectured me about not talking to strangers, but I was lost, desperate, frightened. I wanted to go home, and he promised that he would take me there. I told him my name and where I lived. I remember him turning to look at the other man, the one who was driving, and they started laughing. Then he opened the door and got out. The next thing I knew, he grabbed me and shoved me inside the van.

"I knew then that I had made a mistake, and I tried to get away. I started kicking and screaming, begging him to let me go, but he slapped me hard across the face and told me to be quiet. He tied my hands behind my back and my feet together at the ankles, then stuffed a dirty rag into my mouth and forced me down on the floor in the back of the van. I remember gagging at the sour taste on the rag. The van's metal floor was rough and scraped my cheek and knees, making them bleed. I was sure that I was going to die, that they were going to kill me.''

She drew in a long, shuddery breath, before she could continue. '''They drove into the mountains, dragged me inside a cabin and locked me in the bedroom, my hands and feet still tied. There was a small gap between the curtains. Just a narrow slit in which I could see the branches of a tree, a slice of sky.''

She angled her head to peer at the window across the room and the dark view beyond the glass. ''I heard the men talking, knew that they planned to demand a ransom for me from my parents. I was scared that my mother and father would be angry with me for running away and wouldn't give the men the money they wanted. With each passing day, I was convinced that was the case.''

Link didn't want to hear her answer, was sure that he wouldn't be able to bear it if she confirmed his fears, but found himself asking, ''Did the men...hurt you?''

She turned to look at him, then dropped her gaze, obviously understanding what he was asking. ''No. Not in that way. They shoved me around quite a bit. Teased me. But they never touched me. Not sexually.''

Relief spilled through him in waves, but he did his best to keep the emotion from his expression.

She lifted her face again to meet his gaze. "The police worked closely with my parents, advised them every step of the way. They set up taps on all the phones. In our home, and at my father's company, too. Once the call came, they made arrangements with the bank for the marked bills to be offered for my ransom. Of course, I didn't know any of this at the time. I only knew what I could hear through the closed door. The men were drinking and they would argue violently with each other over how and where the money was to be exchanged, what they would do and where they would go once they had it. I knew that even if they did get the money, they would kill me. I heard them talk about it. How they would do it."

She sank back on her heels, drawing her hands together on her thighs, linking them tightly as she stared down at them. She drew in a breath and released it slowly, letting it shudder out of her. "I'd be dead today, if someone hadn't tipped off the police. An anonymous call," she said, lifting her face to look at him again. "Someone called and told the police who had me and where they could find me. But whoever it was never came forth to claim the reward my parents had offered for information about my abduction."

She shook her head, as if to clear the oddity of that. "I'll never forget the morning the police burst in. It was the day my parents were supposed to make the drop. The men were asleep in the front room. It was early. Just after dawn. I could hear birds singing in the trees outside the window. Then, suddenly, the birds stopped singing and everything grew quiet. It seemed as if even the wind stilled. There was only the sound of the men's snores coming from the front room. I sensed that something was different, that something was about to happen, but didn't know what. Then there was an explosion, glass shattering, wood splintering. Shouts. Grunts. I remember screaming. Closing my eyes and just screaming.

"The bedroom window behind me shattered and glass sprayed across the floor, pelted the mattress, stinging my legs. I opened my eyes then, and saw a man crawling through the window. He had on a mask. A gas mask, though I didn't know what it was at the time.

"The man was dressed in black, and he had all this equipment strapped to him. He held a gun, a rifle of some kind, against his chest and he dropped down on a knee beside me. I was terrified. I wasn't sure whether he was there to kill me or rescue me. He pulled another mask from a belt at his waist and put it over my face, then picked me up and carried me to the window. He passed me through the opening, handing me to another man who waited outside. I remember my first gulp of air," she said, and closed her eyes, drew in a long, deep breath, as if even now she could savor it. She released the breath on a sigh. "Fresh. Clean. After smelling nothing but sour bodies and whiskey and the musty mattress for three days, it was glorious. As if freedom had a scent."

She grew quiet, her eyes misting.

"And the men?" he prodded.

She returned her gaze to his and her lips trembled. "They were captured. Put in prison. There was never a question of their guilt. Plus it was discovered that they were guilty of other crimes, which added additional years to the sentences each received." She turned her face to the window again and hugged her arms around her waist, her expression taking on a haunted look. "I've always feared that they would get out," she confessed quietly. "Escape. Come and find me. Kill me as they had planned to do."

Link saw the shiver that shook her and reached for her, drawing her back to his side. Tucking her head beneath his chin, he pressed his lips against her hair. "They won't get out," he said, his voice husky. "I promise you. Those men will never hurt you again."

Link knew because he'd made it his business to know, to be present each time the prisoners' cases came up for review. The other crimes the men had committed had added years on to those assessed for Isabelle's kidnapping. The two would be old men before they became eligible for release. And, if there was such a thing as justice, the two wouldn't live long enough to see outside prison walls again.

# Three

Isabelle awakened slowly, her mind first, lazily shuffling through the sensations that floated around her like a heavy mist. She felt as if she were snuggled in a cocoon. Safe, warm, protected, cushioned. Such an unusual feeling. So unlike anything she'd ever felt before. She stretched contentedly, enjoying the euphoric feeling—and bumped something hard with her knee. She blinked open her eyes in surprise...and found herself staring into Link Templeton's sleeping face.

Swallowing a shocked gasp, she stared, the memories of the previous night slowly unfolding in her mind. The nightmare. The terror that had gripped her. The screams tearing through her throat. The haunting memories. Link holding her, comforting her. Telling him about the kidnapping. The sense of release she'd felt to at last be able to share with someone the horror of it all. The strength in the arms that had wound around her, being drawn to a chest hard with muscle, her cheek pillowed by the mat of soft, dark hair that swirled there. The musky smell of his skin beneath her nose. The warmth of his flesh seeping into hers, chasing away the chilling fear. Her eyes growing heavy. Sleeping.

And now, hours later, he still held her. He had one arm draped loosely over her waist. The other was pinned beneath her head, a wide palm curved around the base of her neck. He'd flung one leg across hers, the weight of it a pleasant burden. His scent surrounded her, filled her. That rich, heady, musky male scent that charged her senses with each careful breath she drew.

She shuddered a sigh and snuggled closer, but kept her face tipped up to his, studying the angles, the planes, the scars there. One ran from the corner of his mouth, less than an inch long. A faint line, almost indiscernible unless one looked closely, as she was now. A second scar creased his forehead. A permanent worry line, she decided, just managing to resist the urge to trace it with the tip of a finger. There was a crook in his nose. A slight one. And she found herself wondering if he'd broken it in the line of duty, or perhaps in a fight.

He looked like the type who might have engaged in a brawl or two, before crossing over to the side of the law. Perhaps in his youth? There was a toughness about him, a cocky swagger to his walk, that made her think of a high school bad boy. But this was no boy's face she looked upon. This was the face of a man. Creases fanned from the corners of his eyes, permanent squint lines that only intensified already ruggedly handsome features. A heavy shadow of beard darkened his jaw and the narrow space between his upper lip and nose. She wondered what it would feel like to brush her lips across the stubble. Rough? Coarse? Would it tickle…or entice?

Shivering deliciously at the thought, she tucked her hands beneath her cheek to keep from testing her theory with at least a touch. She knew it was probably wrong to stare so openly, so lustfully, but what harm would it do? He was asleep and would never know…and her curiosity would finally be satisfied.

She'd wondered about him, dreamed about him, since that first day she'd seen him after returning to Pueblo from Europe. He'd been standing in front of the courthouse, one hand shoved deeply into his slacks pocket, the other rubbing at the base of his neck, as if easing knots of tension there.

She had watched him unobserved from her car, absolutely spellbound by his rugged good looks, his mouthwatering physique. The wide shoulders, narrow waist that tapered to even slimmer hips, sturdy, muscled legs. But then he'd turned his back to her and walked away, and she'd nearly lost her breath. With his hand still thrust deeply into his pocket, his slacks were pulled tight across his backside, emphasizing firm, rounded buttocks, muscled thighs. His stride was purposeful, confident…his very posture seeming to dare anyone to defy him.

She'd lost her heart that day. As foolishly and carelessly as a young schoolgirl, she'd fallen deeply and madly in love. And with a stranger, no less. But she'd discovered his identity soon after, in a conversation with her brother Riley. They'd been at a political function, one of those boring fund-raisers that her parents attended faithfully. She'd seen him standing at the end of the bar, looking positively rakish, dressed in a collarless black silk shirt and black slacks with flat, precise pleats at the waist. He'd looked as bored as she, scanning the room with a narrowed, jaundiced eye. His disapproval of the people gathered there—or the event, she was never sure which—was obvious in the derisive slant of his mouth.

Though she'd been attracted to Link from the first moment she'd seen him, her lack of experience with men had made her hesitant to seek an introduction. And once they had been formally introduced, his cool indifference toward her had dashed any hopes that she might have clung to that the attraction wasn't all one-sided.

Not long after their introduction, she'd begun to date Brad. Her fanciful dreams of Link should have ended with her engagement to Brad, but they hadn't. She continued to dream of him almost nightly, wonderful dreams in which he'd hold her close while kissing her passionately.

At the thought of kissing him, she caught her lower lip between her teeth. Did she dare do so now? Would he awaken, if she did? To test the depth of his sleep, she drew a hand from beneath her cheek and touched two fingers lightly to his chest. When he didn't flinch, or respond in any way, she increased the pressure, stroking her fingertips down between the twin pads of muscle on his bare chest, thrilling at the warmth of his skin, the softness of the hair that curled round her fingers.

When still he didn't move, she grew braver and lifted her head. She drew in a long, nervous breath, then leaned to touch her lips to his. She withdrew, shivered deliciously at the taste, the textures she'd found there, and glanced up at his eyes. They were still shuttered, his lashes twin shadows brushing his cheeks.

Unable to resist, she leaned into him again, taking her tongue in a slow journey across the crease of his lips. She froze when his lips parted on a ragged sigh, his breath blowing warm and moist against her face. He shifted, hauled her hips closer to his. She remained frozen, paralyzed by fear, staring at his closed lids, waiting for them to open. When they remained closed, when his breathing returned to the steady rhythm of sleep, she all but melted with relief.

Nervously, she slicked her lips, wetting them, hesitated a moment longer, then raised them to meet his again. This time his response was immediate and thrilling. The arm at her waist tightened, drawing her hips hard against his, and his mouth opened beneath hers, his tongue arrowing out to tease hers in a slow, sensual dance. A shiver chased through her, one that fired each nerve and left it burning on its journey to her toes. She felt his manhood lengthen and swell against her abdomen, the slow curl of his fingers dig into her hip...and nearly wept as her bones melted, her mind clouded. A ball of heat formed low in her center, radiated outward, until she felt like one huge ache of long suppressed need. She curled her hands around his neck and drew his face closer.

She'd never kissed a man like this before. Never. Not and felt the way she did right now. All achy and needy, as if she were sure she would die if he stopped…and die if he didn't. Brad's kisses, though passionate, had never left her feeling so heady, so sinfully wanton. But, then, she'd never really liked kissing Brad. Never quite trusted him, either. And it seemed her instincts had been right.

But Link…

She'd dreamed of him, lusted after him in a way that made her blush, even now, as she reflected upon it. She'd spent hours weaving dreams of him holding her, kissing her, making love with her, and in the most exotic places and erotic ways. Not that she knew anything about making love. She didn't. Only what she'd read or seen portrayed on a movie screen. She was a virgin. A fact that had frustrated Brad Rowan. Angered him, even, when she'd refused to sleep with him before they were properly married.

But she'd made love with Link, willingly, if only in her dreams. And he'd been a passionate lover. A satisfying one. Not selfish and demanding, as Brad had been when he'd tried to woo her into his bed. In her dreams, Link's kisses had been gentle, tender, loving, turning hot and passionate. Just as they were now, she thought as his lips swept over hers. She could taste the passion in him, feel the heat that burned beneath the layers of control.

Even as the thought formed, she found herself

dragging her mouth from his. She eased back to stare up at him, her eyes wide in shock. My God! she thought wildly. She'd kissed him, and him her. Link Templeton was lying in bed with her, both of them half dressed, and he was kissing her senseless. The very man who had arrested her brother! But even as the thought formed, she realized that whatever resentment she'd held toward Link for that act was now gone. By his own admission, Link had simply been doing his job in arresting Riley, and it was through his tireless efforts that Riley's name had been eventually cleared.

As she stared, remembering again her wanton actions, he opened his eyes, their hazy color a sleepy, gray-blue as they met hers. She gulped a breath. Swallowed. Afraid to move. Afraid to breathe. Would he be angry that she had kissed him? Repulsed?

"I—I—" Before she could think of an excuse, even a lame one, to offer for her actions, he lifted a hand and laid it on her cheek. She closed her eyes at his touch, the warmth, the tenderness with which his fingers stroked over her skin, making her weak.

"I thought I was dreaming," he said, his voice husky with sleep.

She wanted to laugh, cry, wasn't sure which would come out if she dared open her mouth. Instead, she opened her eyes and simply stared.

"So beautiful," he murmured, tracing just the tips of his fingers along her jaw. "So, so beautiful."

She swallowed. Hard. Opened her mouth, then closed it again, unable to think of a single thing to say in return. She closed her eyes, arching instinctively, needfully as his fingers skimmed down her throat.

"Link," she whispered, her voice trembling, then sucked in a breath when his palm slid down to cover her breast.

"What?" he murmured, shaping his fingers around her breast's fullness and gently kneading.

She gulped, sure that the ball of fire that knotted low in her stomach would burst into flames at any moment and consume them both. "I...I..." She groaned, melting, when he dipped his head and opened his mouth over her breast, warming it with his breath. He flicked his tongue against the turgid nipple that budded beneath the thin silk, making it throb.

"You what?" he murmured.

"I—I knew it would feel like this." She moaned, arching higher, when he nipped at her aching nipple, then soothed it with his tongue. "You. This." She wove her fingers through his hair and closed her eyes, holding him against her. "I imagined it. Dreamed of it. But it's better. So much better than I even dreamt." She moaned, then shivered.

She felt him stiffen and her own body tensed in response. Then he lifted his head and cool air chilled the damp spot he'd left on the silk over her breast. She opened her eyes to meet his...and saw the cold fury that churned there. Stunned by it, she shrank away.

He slid his hand from her breast to her throat and closed his fingers around it. Not painfully, but her eyes widened just the same as the sleepy blue in his eyes turned to flint.

"You were going to marry him," he said, his voice rough with accusation. "Less than twenty-four hours ago, you were going to marry Brad Rowan, yet you are lying here in this bed, making love with me. Why, Isabelle?" he growled, and tightened his fingers around her throat. "How can you love one man, and make love to another?"

She felt the tears spurt to her eyes, felt her throat tighten. "I don't love Brad. I never did."

"But you were going to marry him," he insisted.

"Yes, but only because my parents expected me to."

"Expected you?" he all but shouted at her.

"Yes," she said, blinking back tears. "They thought Brad would make a suitable husband for me. And I wanted to give them the land," she added, desperate to make him understand.

"Land? What land?"

"Lightfoot's Plateau. Brad refused to sell it to my family, but at a dinner one night with my family, he said that he'd give the land to me, as a wedding present, if I'd agree to marry him. I thought that by marrying him, I could give something back to my family. Something to repay them for all the suffering, the pain I had caused them."

He stared at her for what seemed like an eternity, never once moving his gaze from hers. "You'd give yourself to a man in exchange for a piece of land?" He stared at her a moment longer, then snatched his hand from her throat, as if touching her repulsed him, then rolled away from her and to his feet.

The tears she'd held back slipped over her lashes and burned a trail of shame down her cheeks as she watched him stalk away.

"A piece of land," he muttered, then whirled back to glower at her. "You'd trade your heart, your body, to a man for a goddamn piece of real estate?"

Her temper flared to match his, and she pushed herself to a sitting position and swiped angrily at the tears. "You can't possibly understand," she cried furiously. "You wouldn't know what it's like to be pitied, all but smothered, fussed over as if you were a fragile piece of china that might break at the slightest jarring. My parents went through hell when I was kidnapped, both blaming themselves for something that was totally out of their control. And when they were unable to live with the guilt any longer, the fear of it all happening again, they sent me away to boarding school back east."

She flung the quilt from her legs and swung her feet over the side of the bed, her chest heaving as she stood to face him. "I was a child when they sent me away. Felt as if I'd disappointed them, let them down. And every time I came home for a visit, it was the same. I could see it in their eyes. The pity. The regret. The shame. The fear that never seemed to leave them. And when I came home for good, a grown woman, they continued to treat me as a child. Protecting me. Hovering over me. Well, this was my chance to prove to them I was no longer a child, to give them something back. And if I sacrificed my heart, and in doing

so, my body, then so be it. I'd gladly give them my
life for all they've suffered and sacrificed for me.
They sacrificed a life with me, their only daughter,
spent hundreds of thousands of dollars to ensure my
safety while providing me with an excellent education
both back east and abroad.''

Shaking with fury, she waited for a response from
him. Anything. When he continued to stare at her, his
eyes narrowed in anger, his lip curled in disgust, she
whirled for the bathroom, not wanting him to see the
tears of shame that burned behind her eyes.

Link stood before the screen door, his thoughts as
tangled as his emotions, staring out at the landscape
and the evidence of the previous night's storm. Moisture from the rain clung to the leaves, making them
shimmer in the bright sunlight, while murky water
pooled in the ruts that his Blazer had left on the dirt
road leading to the cabin.

Isabelle hadn't loved Brad. She'd told him so herself. She'd agreed to marry him out of a sense of duty.

Duty.

He snorted and lifted a hand to brace it against the
door frame, narrowing his eyes on the view beyond
the door. Link Templeton could write a book on the
sacrifices made from a sense of duty, but not a one
of them had involved his heart, his very soul.

He sensed Isabelle's presence behind him and
glanced over his shoulder to find her standing in the
doorway to the bedroom. She'd changed from her
nightgown and now wore a sundress, its thin straps
exposing creamy shoulders, its hem brushing against

the slender calves of her legs. Her chin was tipped high and there was a rosy flush to her cheeks, sure signs that she was still angry with him.

But anger was good, he told himself as he turned back to stare through the screen door. Much better than the flush of desire he'd seen there earlier. "I'm going to town," he told her.

"I'll get my things," she replied tersely.

"I'm going alone."

He heard her gasp of surprise but ignored it.

"You're leaving me here alone?" she whispered in disbelief.

He rammed a hand in his pocket and pulled out his keys. "Just for a couple of hours." He shoved open the screen door, anxious, desperate to put some distance between them. "Don't make any phone calls while I'm gone," he said, tossing the order over his shoulder. "And stay out of sight."

"But can't I go with you?"

"No." The screen door slammed behind him, an exclamation point to his refusal.

Isabelle paced the main room of the cabin, darting nervous glances at the door, praying that Link would return soon. After he'd left, frightened at the thought of being left alone, she'd locked the door behind him and closed all the windows, pulled the drapes. As a result, the temperature in the cabin was sweltering, the very air stifling. Perspiration beaded her forehead, dampened her skin and trickled irritatingly between her breasts.

She jumped when a noise clattered on the tin roof

overhcad, then groaned, digging her fingers through hair she'd piled on top of her head to relieve the heat. "It's just a pinecone or a twig hitting the roof," she told herself.

Angry with her cowardliness and the fear that ruled her life, she forced herself to cross to the door she'd closed and locked behind Link when he'd left. Fingers trembling, she drew in a deep breath, flipped the lock and pulled open the heavy door. Sunshine flooded into the cabin, warming her already hot face, and nearly blinding her. Laying a palm against the rusted screen, she squinted up at the cloudless blue sky, then down at her wristwatch. An hour. He'd only been gone an hour.

And she'd go mad if she spent one more minute in the stifling cabin alone.

Ever since her kidnapping, she'd never truly been alone. Her parents had seen to that. They'd made arrangements for employees at both the boarding school back east and the finishing school in Europe she'd attended to escort her wherever she needed to go, while relatives and close family friends were recruited to supervisc her holidays and whatever free time she was allowed.

As a result, a fear of aloneness had been as much a part of her education as the study of Socrates and the proper placement of silver for a formal table setting.

But she wouldn't let fear rule her life any longer, she told herself furiously.

Setting her jaw, she pushed open the screen and stepped out onto the narrow porch. Feeling the fear prick at her, she hugged her arms beneath her breasts as she looked out at the circle of trees that surrounded the small cabin. Drawing in long, deep breaths, she forced the tension from her neck, her shoulders, her knees, the paralyzing fear from her body. Determined not to let the fear control her life any longer, she took that first timid step out into the world alone.

Link grabbed from the passenger seat the guest list Hank had provided him with and the sack of groceries he'd purchased, then shouldered open the door of the Blazer. Glancing around as he dropped to the ground, he headed for the cabin. He stepped inside, frowned as the heat struck him like a fist in the face and crossed to the table. He tossed the papers down, dropped the sack to the table, then turned, his frown deepening.

"Isabelle?"

He listened, his heart kicking into a faster beat when he didn't hear a reply, then headed for the bedroom. "Isabelle!" he shouted. The bedroom was dark, the drapes drawn, the bed neatly made. He pushed the bathroom door open, then spun back around, swearing, when he found it empty. He raced for the front door and out onto the porch, forcing himself to stop, think, when he reached its edge. He hadn't met any other vehicles on the way back up the mountain road, he told himself. There was no way anyone could have discovered their hideout, or reached it, without traveling that road.

Or could they?

Cursing himself for leaving her alone, he scanned

the ground, looking for any signs that might indicate that someone, other than himself, had approached the cabin. Seeing nothing, he stepped out into the yard but kept his gaze on the ground. Not more than twenty feet from the cabin's front door, he saw the impression of a footprint on a spot of ground washed free of vegetation. He hunkered down to examine the small indentation, noted its size, then lifted his gaze toward the woods.

Surely she wouldn't have gone off alone, he told himself, even as he rose to follow the faint tracks that led him to the small opening between the trees. The thick branches overhead blocked out the sun, making it difficult, and at times impossible, to see her tracks on the forest floor. But he stuck to the faint path, knowing that there was no way that Isabelle would have been able to pierce the thick undergrowth that crowded both sides of the path to leave it.

With panic nipping at his heels, he jogged through the woods, slapping low-hanging branches out of his way as he played through his mind possible scenarios of what have might have happened while he was gone. The first and most terrifying was that Brad had discovered their hideout and had somehow lured Isabelle into the woods. A second, no less comforting theory, was that she had grown frightened in the cabin alone, and had run away into the woods to hide.

Either way, she was gone, and Link felt responsible.

Swearing under his breath, he broke into a run, his lungs burning as he fought his way higher up the rough path. He wanted to call her name, shout it from the top of his lungs, in hopes she'd answer him, but he kept his lips pressed tightly together, knowing he had to keep his presence a surprise, in the event that Brad did have her.

Up ahead, he heard the sound of running water and pushed himself harder. He broke into a small clearing that opened up beside a mountain stream and stopped, his chest heaving, the muscles in his legs burning. Swollen from the previous night's rain, the stream swept past him in a wild torrent, crashing over rocks and pushing over the banks where the land had washed away. Limbs ripped from trees and other debris gathered by the storm bobbed in the fast-moving current, swept along by its strong force.

A moan rose from deep inside him as he searched the bank for a sign of her. The mournful sound lodged in his throat and burned there as he caught a glimpse of a thin leather strap, peeking from a pile of rocks mounded against the end of a tree trunk that stretched from one side of the bank to the other, creating a natural bridge. His heart pounding, he raced to the edge of the stream, snatched up the sandal and looked across the rushing water and down the far bank. A hundred feet or so downstream, he caught a glimpse of blue fabric, slapping wetly against the chiseled side of a boulder that jutted from the embankment. Recognizing the fabric as that of the dress Isabelle had worn that morning, he dropped the shoe.

His heart pounding, he leaped onto the trunk of the tree and tightrope-walked the length of it, jumping down when he reached the opposite side. He raced along the edge of the stream, batting the clawing vegetation from his face, until he reached the spot where the boulder protruded from the bank.

"Oh, God," he groaned when he saw Isabelle's limp body, stretched out on the jagged length of stone below. Pressing a boot against the boulder, he tested it to make sure it would support his weight before he lowered himself down. He dropped to a knee at her side and laid a hand on her shoulder.

"Isabelle?" he whispered, his voice breaking. He carefully rolled her over and swept back the wet clumps of hair that clung to her face. "Isabelle," he said more insistently, then sat beside her and picked her up, easing her across his lap. Choking on a sob, he hugged her to his chest and buried his face in the curve of her neck. "Oh, God, Isabelle," he cried, gently rocking her. "I shouldn't have left you alone. I should never have left you alone."

Riddled by fear, by guilt, he lifted his head to look down at her, and smoothed her hair away from her face. He saw the lump on her left temple, the blue tinge to her lips, and quickly stripped off his shirt, fearing a concussion and recognizing the signs of shock. Once he had it wrapped around her, he drew her to him again and pressed his cheek against hers, while rubbing his hand up and down her back, trying to warm her chilled skin.

He held her for what seemed like hours before he felt her stir in his arms. His heart hammering against his ribs, he lifted his head and watched, holding his breath, as she blinked open her eyes. Her gaze met his and a frown pleated the skin between her eyes.

"Link?" she whispered weakly, then closed her eyes again.

"No," he ordered sternly, and caught her chin in his hand. "Don't close your eyes, Isabelle. Look at me."

Her eyelashes fluttered, her lids slowly opened. He held her gaze with his.

"My head," she murmured weakly, and lifted her hand.

He caught her wrist before she could touch the swollen skin and drew her hand into his, squeezing it. "It's just a little bump," he said, silently praying that's all it was. "You must have hit your head when you fell into the stream."

She closed her eyes again and groaned, remembering. "I wanted to cross to the other side. On the tree trunk," she said, and wet her lips. "Stooped to take off my sandals." Her forehead furrowed in a frown again. "Something hit me," she said, and stretched a hand across her chest to knead at a bruise he saw already coloring her shoulder. She wet her lips again, then opened her eyes to meet his. "Something hit me," she whispered.

Link saw the question in her eyes, as well as the fear. "Probably just a limb," he answered her. "When you bent over, a limb being washed down by the stream probably struck you, knocking you over, then you hit your head on a rock as the current carried you farther downstream."

Her eyes drifted closed again and the creases on her forehead smoothed. "Yes," she whispered hoarscly, sounding relieved. "That's probably what happened."

Link swallowed hard, then glanced back across the stream, knowing that somehow he had to get her back to the cabin. "I'm going to carry you," he said, then dropped his gaze to look at her again. "It's going to be slow-going. If I jar you too much, or if I should hurt you in any way, just tell me."

She opened her eyes to meet his. "I'm sorry," she murmured tearfully with regret. "I should have stayed in the cabin."

"We'll worry about apologies later," he said gruffly, figuring he had a few of his own to offer.

Kneeling beside the old footed tub, Link dipped his fingers into the bathwater, testing the temperature, then glanced over at Isabelle. She sat on the toilet seat where he'd placed her, shivering, looking very much like a drowned rat. Her dress clung to her wet skin and her hair hung in soggy clumps over shoulders slumped with exhaustion. He shifted and placed a knuckle beneath her chin to lift her face to his. A streak of mud grazed one cheek and was smeared across her forehead. "Think you can manage a bath?" he asked softly.

Her shoulders rose and fell in a weary sigh. "I think so," she murmured.

He stood and took her hand, supporting her as she rose shakily to her feet. "You'll feel better once you're warm and dry," he told her.

"Promise?" she asked doubtfully as she strained to reach over her shoulder for the dress's zipper.

He shook his head, smiling softly at her weakness, and turned her around. "Yeah, I promise." He caught the zipper tab and pulled it down, his smile melting as the dress's thin straps slid over her shoulders and down her arms. She grabbed the front of the garment and clutched it between her breasts…but her back remained exposed to his gaze.

Unable to look away from the creamy, pebbled flesh, he gulped, swallowed, then followed the bumpy line of her spine to the spot where her waist curved in enticingly before swelling out to form her hips. Suddenly feeling weak-kneed himself, he closed his eyes and drew in a deep breath.

"Link?"

He opened his eyes, tried not to look, but was helpless to do anything else, since the bathroom was small and she stood directly in front of him. He had to clear his throat before he could respond. "Yes?"

"I…feel…faint."

He immediately grabbed her elbows and guided her back down to the toilet seat, then dropped down in front of her and forced her head between her knees. "Take slow, deep breaths," he ordered.

She did as instructed, taking three long breaths before daring to raise her head again. Moaning weakly, she let her head fall back to rest against the wall.

Link's gaze froze on the fistful of fabric she clutched between her breasts, the twin mounds of flesh that swelled around it. It was all he could do to keep from burying his face there.

Knowing how dangerous those thoughts were, he

pushed to his feet. "Can you handle things from here?"

She blinked open her eyes, slowly bringing him into focus. "I think so." Holding the dress against her breasts, she stood, and Link shifted in the small space to give her room. But when her knees buckled again, he grabbed her, catching her before she sank to the floor.

"Maybe I better help you," he suggested uneasily.

Nodding, she turned her back to him and released her hold on the dress. Link's hands tightened on her waist as the dress dropped to pool between their feet. Unsure how best to handle the situation, he nudged her toward the edge of the tub.

"My panties," she murmured, and shoved ineffectively at the strip of silk that barely covered her bottom.

Biting back a groan, Link caught the waist of her panties and stripped them quickly down her legs. She stepped out of them as he rose to stand behind her again.

Taking her elbows again, he gave her another nudge. "In you go," he said gruffly, then held on to her while she lifted first one leg, then the other over the edge of the tub. She sank weakly into the water and leaned back, closing her eyes as she let her head rest against the tub's sloped back.

"Think you'll be okay now?" he asked as he watched water lap between her breasts.

"Y-yes. Thank you."

Link stood a moment longer, staring at her nude form visible beneath the clear water, then tore his

gaze away and headed for the door. "I'll just be outside the door. Holler if you need me."

"'Kay," she murmured, and slid lower in the tub.

Link glanced back over his shoulder one last time.
He bit back a moan as he imagined himself crawling
into the tub with her. It took all the strength he could
muster to step through the doorway and close the door
behind him.

# Four

If medals for valor were ever handed out for guarding a witness, Link figured he'd earned his that night. Anybody who could undress a woman with a body as delectable as Isabelle's, help her into a tub, then dress her in a sexy nightie and tuck her into bed without crawling in beside her and taking advantage of the situation, deserved one. No, they deserved a chest full of medals, he told himself, and flopped to his back on the narrow sofa with a frustrated moan.

He tossed an arm over his eyes and willed the tension from his body, one area at a time...although one remained stubbornly taut.

Damn but she was beautiful, he reflected miserably, then stifled a groan as visions of her nude body filled his mind. Even after a dunking in a cold mountain stream, she had to be the sexiest, most desirable woman he'd ever laid eyes on. Those sweet breasts, small but ripe, their dark, rosy centers puckered and tipped high, just begging for a man's lips.

He rubbed the tips of his fingers together, thoughtfully, almost mournfully. They still carried the feel of her flesh. Soft as satin, sleek and firm as it dipped and rose to form curves sexy enough to test any man's control. Long, slender legs. Delicately small, feminine feet. Toenails painted the palest of pinks.

He sighed and dragged his arm from his eyes to stare miserably at the dark ceiling. Damn! Why couldn't she be poor, ugly, at least ten years older and just as jaded as he? Maybe then he wouldn't feel this obligation to keep his hands off her.

"Link?"

He whipped his head to the side at the sound of her voice. "Isabelle?" he said as he squinted against the darkness. He pushed himself to an elbow while he watched her form take shape as she drifted from the shadows and closer to the sofa. "Are you all right?" he asked in concern.

She stepped into the shaft of moonlight that speared through the window above the sofa and he felt that one last remaining bit of tension he hadn't been able to ease grow stiffer. It had been difficult enough to help her into the skimpy nightgown. But seeing her in it now made him want to rip it off her again.

"I can't sleep," she said softly, and took a tentative step closer.

He sat up slowly, gathering the sheet around his waist as he stared up at her. "Is your head hurting?"

"No."

She sank down on the edge of the sofa next to him, and her scent floated across the space between them to tease at his nose, his senses, his willpower. That flowery, sexy scent that he'd learned to associate with her.

He shifted away, putting a little distance between them. "Is there something you need? Something that I can get for you?"

She dipped her head to stare at the hands she'd folded on her lap. "No. I just—" She glanced over at him, and his heart stopped for a minute at the earnestness of her expression, the unmistakable heat in her eyes.

"This morning," she began, then stopped abruptly. She caught her lower lip between her teeth and dropped her gaze again.

"If you're angry about me leaving you here alone," he said, "I'm sorry. But it was best. If I'd taken you with me—"

She shook her head, silencing him, and he frowned as he watched her pluck nervously at the fabric stretched across her knees.

"No. It's not that," she murmured. "I understand why you couldn't take me with you. But I—" She hesitated a moment, then turned her head slightly to look at him. "I'm sorry that I didn't obey you. That I left the cabin. That I fell into the stream and you had to carry me back to the cabin."

He stared at her, unable to take his eyes off her face. She was beautiful. Desirable. And the flush of shame in her cheeks, the shy way she peered at him, only made her more so.

He tore his gaze from hers and cleared his throat. "No harm done," he said gruffly. "No apology needed."

She reached to lay a hand against his arm. "Oh, but there is!"

He glanced down at the hand on his arm, frowning at the contrasts in their skin. Hers porcelain smooth. Dainty. His dark and hairy. Rough.

She drew her hand back and twisted it with her other on her lap. "But I didn't leave to defy you," she said quietly. "I did it because...well, to prove something to myself." She inhaled deeply, then turned to look at him, moonlight revealing only half of her face. The other half remained in shadows. But he could see the earnestness in her expression, the determination to make him understand.

"I was frightened," he heard her say, and made himself focus on what she was telling him. "Ever since the kidnapping, I've—well, I've always been frightened of being alone. I had locked the door and all the windows after you left, and the cabin was stifling. I became angry with myself and my weakness, and I wanted to prove to myself that there was nothing to be afraid of."

She turned her gaze from his to stare at the far wall. "I went outside, and I saw a doe."

He saw the soft smile that curved at her lips, the wonder that lit her eyes, and had to keep his hands gripped around the edge of the cushion to keep from reaching out and touching her.

"She looked so startled, yet so beautiful. So free. I guess I frightened her, because she turned and plunged into the forest. Without thinking, I followed her. It was peaceful in the forest, so quiet. I didn't realize how far I'd walked until I reached the stream. I knew I should go back, but when I saw the tree trunk that stretched across the stream, I couldn't resist crossing it."

She dipped her head, twisting her hands in her lap again, and her hair fell over her shoulder to curtain her face. Link reached out and brushed it back, tucking it behind her ear. He felt the jolt of awareness that shot through her, the kick of her pulse at his touch.

She turned, and he kept his hand there, cupped behind her ear. He watched her tongue slip between her lips, slick over them...and swallowed a groan, imagining that tongue tangling with his.

"Link?" she whispered. "Would you—"

"What?"

She dropped her gaze again. "I...that is...well, this morning, when we were in bed together..."

He swallowed hard, remembering, wondering where she was going with this. "Yeah?" he asked uneasily. "What about it?"

She glanced over at him again and he saw the flush that stained her cheeks, the heat that turned her eyes to smoke.

"I—liked kissing you." She shook her head in frustration, then firmed her lips. "No," she said more purposefully. "I *loved* kissing you."

Link was struck dumb, unsure what to say in response.

"And I'd like to kiss you again."

He stared at her, at the bright spots of color high on her cheeks, felt the nervous tremble of her body, and let out a slow, uneasy breath. "Isabelle," he said carefully, and dropped his hand from behind her ear. "That was a mistake. You caught me off guard." He curled his fingers around the edge of the cushion between them and dug his fingers into it, determined not to touch her again. "If I'd been fully awake, I would never have taken advantage of you in that way."

"Oh, but you didn't," she insisted, and dropped her hand to cover his. "It was *I* who took advantage of you."

The feel of her hand on his, the warmth, the quiver in it, did nothing to strengthen his resolve to keep his own hands off her. "Just the same," he muttered and tugged his hand from beneath hers. "I shouldn't have done what I did."

Tears filled her eyes. "Is it because you find me unattractive? Unappealing?"

He stared at her, unable to believe that she'd think such a thing, then barked a laugh. "Hell, no!"

"Then why don't you want to kiss me again?"

He puffed his cheeks, blowing out a long breath as he rubbed a hand across the back of his neck and the sudden tension there. "Isabelle. I'm thirteen years older than you."

She cocked her head and frowned at him in puzzlement. "So?"

Frustrated that she wouldn't accept that answer as reason enough and leave him the hell alone, he rose, yanking the sheet around his waist to cover his nudity. "We're from different worlds," he told her, striding away. "I wouldn't know how to treat a woman as gentle and refined as you."

"I won't break."

At the resentment in her tone, he turned to peer at her in surprise. She rose and took a step toward him.

"You're just like my parents and my brothers," she said, her tone now accusing. "You think I need protecting. That I'm a china doll that will shatter at the slightest provocation." She stopped with only inches separating them. "Well, I won't," she informed him stubbornly. "I'm a woman, the same as any other, with the same needs, the same desires."

He reached out to grasp her elbows, intending to hold her away from him, to keep her from drawing any closer. He saw the stubborn glint in her eye, the spark of rebellion there, and wondered if he was strong enough to resist it. "I'm sure you are, Isabelle," he said patiently. "But I'm not the man to—"

His jaw sagged when she reached for the string that dangled between her breasts and gave it a yank, then choked on a startled breath when the panels of silk fell open, exposing the swollen sides of her breasts and the shadowed valley between.

He took a step back, his hands still gripped on her elbows, his fingers digging deep. "Isabelle," he warned. "No."

"Yes," she insisted and shrugged the thin straps from her shoulders. The straps slid down her arms to drop over his hands, exposing her breasts fully.

He stared at the milky-white mounds, the dark centers tipped high as if daring him to touch them. He swallowed hard and shook his head. "No. It's the lump you took on the head. You're not thinking clearly.''

She took a step forward, pressing herself against him. ''There's nothing wrong with what I'm thinking. I want to make love with you.''

''But—''

She took his hand and pressed it over a breast, held it there as she lifted her face to his. ''I've never felt like I did when you kissed me, when you touched me,'' she told him. ''All achy and needy.'' She rose to flick her tongue against the bow of his lips, then sighed, her voice dropping to a sultry drawl. ''So hot I thought I'd burn right up.''

''Isabelle…''

''Kiss me, Link,'' she begged softly, warming his lips with her breath. ''Just kiss me.''

On a low groan, he crushed his mouth over hers, losing his battle for control. And how could he expect to win? he asked himself helplessly as her taste rushed through him like a drug, making him weak, crazy. How could he resist taking what she so freely offered? What he'd wanted, lusted for, for almost a year?

He hooked an arm around her waist, dragged her up hard against him. And took.

She gave readily, parting her lips for him, tangling her fingers in his hair. And when he groaned, she rose higher on her toes and captured his head between her hands, forcing his face closer, the kiss deeper. He staggered a slow circle, already drunk with her taste, his blood pumping fire through his veins, and nudged her back toward the sofa. When the back of her knees struck the cushion, he bent her backward and followed her down. He tore his mouth from hers, buried his face in her neck, drew in a ragged breath, then on a sigh, slid his lips down to capture a nipple between his teeth. When she moaned, arched against him, he opened his mouth over the dark, rosy center and drew her in.

He'd dreamed of this, he reminded himself, spent nights thinking of nothing else. Of her. Of making love to her. But nothing had prepared him for the reality of it, the sweetness, the pleasure, of having his mouth filled with her satiny flesh, of having her body pinned beneath his. He cupped a hand around her breast's fullness, tipped it higher and withdrew to lave her engorged nipple with his tongue.

He glanced up at her over his brows, saw that her eyes were on him, the violet irises a dark, sultry purple, glazed with passion. "Is this what you wanted?" he asked huskily before sucking her deeply into his mouth again.

She filled her hands with his hair and dropped her head back, moaning. "Yes," she whispered. "Ye-e-es," she hissed.

He ripped the sheet from around his waist and tossed it aside, then dragged the nightgown tangled at her waist down her legs and threw it to the floor. He rocked his hips over hers, forcing her legs wider apart until he'd created a nest for himself. "And this?" he asked, pressing his arousal against her.

"Oh, yes," she groaned, knotting her fingers in his hair. She arched against him, demanding, needing more.

Wanting the same, but knowing if he took her now,

he would do so greedily, selfishly, without a thought for her own needs, he braced his hands on either side of her face and lifted his upper body from hers. He stared down at her, his blood pumping wildly through his veins, but couldn't stop the slow smile that bloomed inside him and spread across his face at the disappointment he saw register in her eyes at his withdrawal.

She lifted a hand to press a fingertip against his lips. "What?" she asked, her answering smile hesitant, curious and totally endearing.

"Nothing. Everything." He swooped down to steal a quick kiss. "We're going to do this right," he said, and pushed himself off her and to his feet.

She crossed her arms over her breasts. "Right?"

Charmed by her sudden shyness, he laughed and scooped her up and into his arms. "Yes, right. In bed," he told her, and headed there. He tossed her down onto the mattress, making her squeal, then followed her down, stretching out across her length and burying his face in her neck again. "You smell so sweet," he murmured, and turned his lips against her skin. "And taste sweet, too. Especially right here," he said, and nibbled at the tender flesh at her throat.

She laughed self-consciously as she combed her fingers through his hair. "Are you sure it wasn't *you* who received the lump on the head?"

Surprised by the doubt in her voice, he lifted his head to peer down at her. "You have no idea, do you?"

"What?" she asked, frowning slightly.

"How beautiful you are. How absolutely irresistible."

Color rose to stain her cheeks. "No, I'm not," she murmured, dropping her gaze to his chest.

He pushed himself up on an elbow to stare down at her. "My God," he said in amazement. "You really don't know, do you?"

She wove a finger self-consciously through the hair on his chest. "I don't know what I'm supposed to say to you. No one has ever said anything like that to me before."

He dropped his elbow to lie with his face level with hers again, wondering at the men in her past. Their stupidity. "They should have," he said softly. "Because you are." When she refused to look at him, he caught the hand she held at his chest and squeezed, forcing her gaze to his. "You *are* beautiful," he told her firmly, "and totally irresistible."

She sputtered a self-conscious laugh, dipped her chin, then snuck another peek at his face before dropping her gaze again. "You don't have to say things like that. It isn't as if you have to sweet-talk me into bed. I'm already here."

Delighted by her total lack of womanly wiles, he laughed and grabbed her, rolling to his back and her onto his stomach. "Yeah, you are, aren't you?" He bussed her a quick kiss, then nuzzled his nose against hers. "I just hope you don't regret it," he said, suddenly feeling as insecure as she obviously was.

Her head popped up and she peered down at him, her expression stricken. "Oh, no!" she cried. "Never."

Threading his fingers through her hair, a sardonic smile curved at one corner of his mouth. "Don't be so sure," he warned her. "Morning does something to a person. Sheds a whole new light on things."

"I won't be sorry." She sank back down over his chest and pressed her lips against his heart. "No matter what."

Though he'd brought her to the bedroom to slow things down, to regain a control he was quickly losing, Link realized that it was a wasted effort. There was something about her—her innocence, her total lack of any female vanity, or perhaps it was the tenderness with which she pressed her lips over his heart—that made need swell inside him, a wild animal, demanding release. He dived his fingers through her hair and drew her face close to his, his eyes dark with warning as he searched her gaze. "If you are, it'll be your own damn fault," he told her.

When she opened her mouth to reassure him again, he crushed his over it, rolled, then held her beneath him. Digging his knees into the mattress, he found her moist center, pressed his sex against it. Then, with his hands fisted in her hair, holding her mouth to his, he growled low in his throat and thrust inside her.

She screamed, the sound filling his mouth, echoing inside him, as she arched away from him. He froze, every muscle tensing in denial as he realized too late his mistake.

She was a virgin. God help him. Isabelle was a virgin.

He sagged against her and buried his face against

the side of her neck. "No," he groaned, fisting his hands in her hair. "No!" he raged.

He felt the tremble of her body beneath his, tasted the salt of her tears as they slid down her cheek and over her jaw to wet his lips. Slowly he lifted his head to peer down at her. "Why didn't you tell me?" he asked, his voice raw with regret.

She looked at up him, her eyes brimming with tears. "Because I was afraid you'd say no. That you wouldn't want me."

He groaned again and dropped his forehead against hers. "Issie," he murmured, his voice laden with guilt. "If you'd told me, I would have been more careful with you. I wouldn't have hurt you."

Her palms framed his face and pushed, forcing his head up until their gazes met. "But you didn't hurt me," she told him stubbornly, blinking back tears that indicated he had. "At least, it doesn't hurt anymore." She stroked her thumbs beneath his eyes and a smile trembled at her lips. "I've wanted you, this, ever since I first saw you."

He frowned, searching her face. "What? When?"

She shook her head. "It doesn't matter." She wrapped her arms around his neck. "Just love me, Link. Please?"

When he didn't move, but continued to stare down at her, she lifted her hips and gasped as his still-stiff sex shot deeper inside her. "Ye-e-es," she said, sighing, closing her eyes on a low, pleasure-filled moan. She opened them and the heat he saw there seared through him.

He lifted his hips, intent on drawing away from her,

but she stubbornly followed. Lifted higher, and her velvet walls clamped tightly around him, holding him inside. Need burned through him as he watched the passion wash over her face, felt the soft purr of pleasure that hummed through her.

Lost, he eased back down, thrusting slower this time...and bit back a groan when she arched against him, instead of away.

"Come with me," he urged, sliding a hand beneath her hips. Holding her to him, keeping his strokes slow and easy, he guided her in a dance as old as time, one partnered by a sweetness, an innocence so pure it made his heart twist painfully in his chest, squeezing out tears of regret at his own jadedness.

He brought her to the edge, held her there a rapturous moment, glorying in the feel of her sheathed around him, the desperate dig of her fingers into his neck. Then pushed her over, tumbled after her, his arms locked tightly around her, holding her, his breath tangling with hers, their mouths joined even as their souls became one.

Link lay propped against the pillows, an arm draped low on Isabelle's hip, stroking a thumb over her warm flesh, watching as she pored over the long list of names.

He still couldn't believe that he'd slept with her, taken her virginity. He, the man who had dedicated his entire life to fighting the wrong done to her as a child, had robbed her of the last of her innocence. Her virginity. But when he'd awakened earlier that morning to find her snuggled against him, and with a

smile on her face, he'd been surprised. He was sure
that she would hate him when morning came...or at
the very least, have a few regrets.

Yet, she didn't appear to have a one. In fact, she
seemed almost radiant. Giddy, even. She'd insisted
on making coffee and bringing it to him in bed, along
with the list of wedding guests. She hadn't bothered
with a robe and seemed totally at ease with her nudity, and with his as she served him his coffee, then
settled down beside him to read through the list of
names.

A slight frown puckered between her brows as she
carefully studied each one. When she reached the last,
she tossed down the pages and flopped back against
the pillows beside him. "It's hopeless," she said miserably.

"Nothing struck a chord? A memory?"

She shook her head and leaned forward to gather
the pages back into a neat stack. Sinking back again,
she dropped them onto her lap. "Nothing," she said,
and folded her arms beneath her breasts, her lips
pursed in a pout.

"Maybe you're trying too hard," he suggested, distracted momentarily by the rosy nipple that peeked
from beneath her arm.

She caught her lower lip between her teeth and
worried it. "They're there," she said as if to herself.
"Their names have to be there. The two men were
wedding guests, and my parents had the ushers check
invitations before seating each guest."

He picked up the papers and scanned the first page,
arching a brow when he recognized a few names.

"Isn't he a movie director?" he asked, pointing to one.

She glanced down at the paper, then away, lifting an indifferent shoulder. "Yes. He's an old friend of the family."

He shook his head and flipped the page, noting a couple of more names from the film industry, as well as a few high-ranking politicians. "Do you know all of these people?" he asked in amazement.

She lifted a shoulder again. "Most. Although not well. They're friends and business associates of my parents."

He shook his head and tossed down the papers, reminded again of the gap that yawned between them. One that couldn't be closed. Something that he was going to have to convince her of soon. She snuggled against his side and he dropped a hand over her abdomen, frowning as he splayed his fingers over it, a new worry rising to niggle at his conscience. "Isabelle?" he asked uneasily.

She sighed and snuggled closer. "What?"

"Are you...what I mean to say is, are you...?"

She peered up at him, then smiled. "Yes," she assured him, obviously aware of his sudden, if overdue concern. "I'm on the pill."

Though he tried his best to hide it, his relief must have been obvious, because she laughed and crawled onto his lap to straddle him. She braced her hands against his chest and leaned close, pushing her face within an inch of his. "Were you afraid that you might have gotten me pregnant?" she teased.

"Well, it was a possibility," he said, feeling the

panic lick at him at the mere thought. "We sure as hell didn't take any precautions."

She brushed her lips sensually across his. "No, we didn't," she murmured, then dipped her head to press a kiss into the middle of his chest. She leaned back and smoothed a finger over the moisture she'd left there, then slid her fingers down his stomach. "I'm getting that feeling again," she said, and shot him a wicked look over her brow.

He jerked instinctively as her fingers closed around him, then groaned. "Isabelle—"

She laughed at the strangled sound he made as she stroked her fingers downward, then leaned into him and pressed her mouth against his. "What's the matter, Link?" she teased.

He reared back to look at her, unable to believe the change in her. What had happened to the shy, innocent woman who had barely been able to look him in the eye the day before? And where had this bold temptress come from?

He groaned as her fingers stroked back up, and he flipped her to her back, wondering why he was even questioning the change.

"Better watch it," he warned. "Keep that up and you might get more than you bargained for."

She arched a brow as she stroked her fingers to the base of his sex. "Promise?" she asked coyly, then curled her fingers around him and guided him to her.

He jerked violently as the sensitive tip of his sex met her warm, moist opening. "Isabelle," he gasped, then set his jaw, stifling a shuddering groan as he slid inside her.

Smiling, she stroked her palms down his back. "What's wrong?" she asked innocently as she molded her hands over his buttocks and shifted, drawing his hips closer to hers.

Gasping, he closed his eyes and dropped his forehead against hers. He inhaled deeply, once… twice…three times, before he released the breath in a ragged sigh and replied, "Nothing." He drew back to meet her gaze and returned her smile. "Absolutely nothing."

Bracing his hands at either side of her head, he thrust deeply, watching her eyes shoot wide, her breath catch in her throat. "Something wrong?" he asked, feigning the same innocence she had.

Unable to speak, she dug her fingers deeply into the flesh of his buttocks and shook her head. "No," she assured him, then gulped a breath. "Nothing."

He grinned as he pushed himself deeper inside. "Are you sure?"

"Yes," she gasped, arching to meet him, then cried, "No!" and attempted to hold him against her when he began to withdraw. "Please," she begged. "Again."

He dipped his head low and captured a nipple between his teeth. "Again what?" he asked, teasing the bud to life with his tongue.

"Oh, yes," she gasped as he closed his mouth over her breasts and began to suckle. "There. And there," she cried when he pushed his sex deeper inside her. She squeezed her eyes shut, arching against him, then opened them to scorch him with the heat that burned there. "Love me," she begged almost desperately.

She reached for him, framing his face between her hands, and drew his mouth to hers. "Love me," she said again as she touched her lips to his.

Link melted at her words, knowing that he had little choice but to love her, then, just as quickly, he stiffened as she mated her tongue with his and her taste rushed through him, clouding his mind, filling his soul, heating his blood. He gathered her hands in his and pushed them up over her head, holding them there as he stretched out, matching his length to hers. With his mouth welded to hers, he pushed deeper inside her, feeling the pressure build around him with each new thrust. Heat pulsed between them, coating their bodies with a fine sheen of perspiration, and adding a friction to their joining. He felt her body tense beneath his, felt the wild thrust of her body against his. And he froze, holding himself still as she came apart around him. He gloried in the sensations that poured through his body, was blinded by the emotion that stung his eyes.

Never in his life had he experienced anything like this. Like her. Never had he felt so completely joined with a woman, as if their bodies, their hearts, their very souls were one. The realization weakened him, even as it thrilled him.

"Isabelle," he groaned, then set his jaw and thrust one last time, crying out her name as he found his own trembling release within her.

His chest heaving, he released her hands to gather her into his arms. "Issie," he murmured breathlessly, as he rolled to his back, taking her with him. "My Issie," he said, as he held her against his heart.

* * *

That same afternoon, Link strode into headquarters and headed straight for his desk, hoping to get the file he needed and make a quick exit, before anyone noticed his presence.

A few heads lifted as he pulled open the file drawer with a screech of metal, but he pretended not to notice as he flipped through the folders crammed inside.

"Templeton!"

He stifled a groan, plucked out the file he wanted, then slammed the drawer. "Yeah, boss?" he called, glancing toward the chief's office door.

"Inside," the chief growled.

Inhaling deeply, Link tucked the folder beneath his arm and strode for the doorway. He squeezed past Chief Luben, who remained stubbornly in the doorway, glowering at him, then waited while his superior closed the door and moved to stand behind his desk.

"Where the hell have you been?" Luben growled.

Link lifted a noncommittal shoulder. "Chasing down leads."

Luben's eyes narrowed. "What leads?"

"On the Dodd murder case. It's still our priority, right?"

Luben swelled his chest and a vein pulsed to life at his temple. "Was. We've got a bigger problem on our hands right now, one that you'd be privy to," he added, leveling a sausagelike finger at Link's nose, "if you bothered to check in on a regular basis."

Link tried to keep his expression impassive. "You've never found fault with my work habits before."

The chief's hand came down on the desk hard,

making the phone rattle and papers fly. "That was because I've never had Fortune breathing down my neck. His daughter's disappeared, and all we've got to go on so far is a wrecked car we found this morning abandoned out in the desert."

Link pulled at his chin, pretending to absorb the details he'd heard, playing for time. He needed to know Rowan's reaction to Isabelle's disappearance, his movements since he'd left the church. And in order to gather that information, he would have to bring Rowan's name into the conversation.

But that was going to be difficult, since no one but himself and Hank knew that Brad Rowan was a suspect in Mike Dodd's murder. Neither of them had been foolish enough to breathe a word of their suspicions to the chief or anyone else in the department. Not when they didn't have a shred of evidence to substantiate their claim. Not when their prime suspect was a prominent businessman in Pueblo. Not when the suspect was the son of one of the town's leaders.

"What about her fiancé?" he asked, keeping his expression carefully schooled.

The chief snorted. "Rowan? He's raging around town like a bull, threatening to kill whoever abducted her."

Link arched a brow. "Abducted?"

Luben scowled and picked up a file folder, then tossed it down again. "What other explanation could there be? Naturally, her family is worried. You know the girl's history, don't you?"

"Yeah, I do. But what makes Rowan think she's been abducted? Maybe she just got cold feet."

The chief snorted again and rounded the desk. He propped a hip on the corner and braced his hands on his thigh. "If that's the case, then where is she? Why wouldn't she tell her family her location when she called them, and who she's with? And how do you explain the wrecked car?"

"Have you brought it in?"

Luben waved a dismissing hand. "Yeah. Towed it in this morning. The lab guys are going over it now."

Link tensed, thinking of the fingerprints he'd left on Isabelle's car when he'd rescued her from it.

The chief narrowed his eyes at him. "I want you to take the lead on this, Templeton. I know you and Fortune had words when you arrested Riley, but you're the best I've got, and I need you on this case."

Link inhaled deeply, already trying to figure out a way he could keep his own involvement in Isabelle's disappearance from being discovered. "No problem, boss." He touched a finger to his brow in a mock salute. "I'll go take a look at the car now."

Link stepped into the garage, paused a moment to let his eyes adjust to the change in light, then strode straight for Isabelle's red sports car, parked in a bay. Both doors were open and a pair of legs stuck out from the driver's side. As Link walked, he played the scene from the car wreck back through his mind, trying to remember his exact movements, everywhere he'd placed a hand when he'd pulled Isabelle from the vehicle. Everywhere he'd left a print.

Forcing a smile, he ducked his head inside the car and braced one hand against the back of the seat and the other on the steering wheel. "Hey, Smitty," he said, bumping a knee against the tech's leg. "Hear we've got us a missing lady."

Smitty reared up, swearing, when he struck his head on the rearview mirror. "Dammit, Link!" he said, giving Link's chest an angry shove. "Have you lost your mind? Can't you see I'm dusting for prints here?"

Link lifted his hands in surrender and backed away from the interior of the car. "Sorry, Smitty. Thought you'd be through by now."

Smitty scowled and wiggled from inside the car to his feet, ripping off his gloves. "Not when a Fortune's involved. Hell! I'll be lucky if I finish before five. Damn their rich hides. They've got everybody on the force jumping through hoops." He tossed the gloves toward a waste receptacle, missed and swore again.

Link stepped back as Smitty stomped over to retrieve them. Though a slob when it came to his own appearance, Smitty ran a tight ship. He considered the garage his own personal territory and kept it as sterile as any surgical suite. Not a trace of grease on the floor, not so much as a lug wrench out of place. "Find anything, yet?" he asked innocently as he watched Smitty scoop the gloves from the cement floor.

Smitty slam-dunked the gloves into the receptacle, then spun back around, yanking a Laker's ball cap from his head to dig his fingers through his hair. "Not yet. I really just got started. They had me at the church all day yesterday and this morning, dusting every cross and doorknob in the place."

Link grinned, and clapped Smitty on the back. "Go to confession while you were there?"

Smitty scowled and rammed his hands into the back pockets of his overalls. "Like I've got anything to confess," he muttered cantankerously. "They don't give me enough time off from here to even think about sinning."

Link laughed and stepped back, draping a casual arm along the top edge of the car door. "You'd just get in trouble if they did."

"I could use a little trouble," Smitty grumped. "Hell!" he said, tossing up a hand. "I haven't had a hard-on in a week, much less relieved one."

Link dropped his arm from the car, shaking his head sympathetically as he reached for the door handle. "Don't let me keep you then. I know you've got—"

"Don't—" Smitty dropped his head back on a groan as Link's fingers curled around the handle "—touch that," he finished miserably.

Link jerked his hand back, but not before smearing the prints there. "Sorry," he muttered as he backed away from the car. Then he grinned and gave Smitty a playful punch on the arm. "But at least you'll know how my prints got on the car, right?"

Smitty scowled and tugged another pair of sterile gloves out of the box he'd propped on the car's trunk. "You just better hope I find someone other than yours," he muttered. "Otherwise, we're *both* going to be up to our eyeballs in trouble."

Mission accomplished, Link thought wearily as he climbed from the Blazer well after dark. He'd made

# PLAY "LUCKY 7" AND GET
# THREE FREE GIFTS!

## HOW TO PLAY:

1. With a coin, carefully scratch off the silver box at the right. Then check the claim chart [to] see what we have for you — **2 FREE BOOKS** and a gift — **ALL YOURS! ALL FREE!**

2. Send back this card and you'll receive two brand-new Silhouette Desire® novels. The[se] books have a cover price of $3.99 each in the U.S. and $4.50 each in Canada, but they a[re] yours to keep absolutely free.

3. There's no catch. You're und[er] no obligation to buy anything. [We] charge nothing — ZERO — [for] your first shipment. And you do[n't] have to make any minimum numb[er] of purchases — not even one!

4. The fact is thousands of readers enjoy receiving their books by mail from the Silhoue[tte] Reader Service.™ They enjoy the convenience of home delivery...they like getting the b[est] new novels at discount prices, BEFORE they're available in stores...and they love their *He[art] to Heart* newsletter featuring author news, horoscopes, recipes, book reviews and much mo[re.]

5. We hope that after receiving your free books you'll want to remain a subscriber. B[ut] the choice is yours — to continue or cancel, any time at all! So why not take us up on o[ur] invitation, with no risk of any kind. You'll be glad you did!

## YOURS FREE!

### PLAY LUCKY 7 FOR THIS EXCITING FREE GIFT!

*THIS SURPRISE
MYSTERY GIFT
COULD BE
YOURS FREE WHEN
YOU PLAY*

## LUCKY 7!

Visit us online at
www.eHarlequin.com
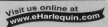

PLAY THE

## LUCKY 7

SLOT MACHINE GAME!

Just scratch off the silver box with a coin. Then check below to see the gifts you get!

# YES!

I have scratched off the silver box. Please send me the 2 FREE books and gift for which I qualify. I understand I am under no obligation to purchase any books, as explained on the back and opposite page.

326 SDL C6NA

225 SDL C6M6
(S-D-OS 12/00)

NAME                (PLEASE PRINT CLEARLY)

ADDRESS

APT.#        CITY

STATE/PROV.              ZIP/POSTAL CODE

| 7 7 7 | WORTH TWO FREE BOOKS PLUS A BONUS MYSTERY GIFT! |
| cherries | WORTH TWO FREE BOOKS! |
| clubs | WORTH ONE FREE BOOK! |
| bells | TRY AGAIN! |

# The Silhouette Reader Service™ — Here's how it works:

Accepting your 2 free books and gift places you under no obligation to buy anything. You may keep the books and gift and return the shipping statement marked "cancel." If you do not cancel, about a month later we'll send you 6 additional novels and bill you just $3.34 each in the U.S., or $3.74 each in Canada, plus 25¢ shipping & handling per book and applicable taxes if any.* That's the complete price and — compared to cover prices of $3.99 each in the U.S. and $4.50 each in Canada — it's quite a bargain! You may cancel at any time, but if you choose to continue, every month we'll send you 6 more books, which you may either purchase at the discount price or return to us and cancel your subscription.

*Terms and prices subject to change without notice. Sales tax applicable in N.Y. Canadian residents will be charged applicable provincial taxes and GST.

an appearance at headquarters, bluffed his way through a confrontation with the chief and dealt with the prints he'd left on Isabelle's car. Not bad for an afternoon's work.

But the reprieve he'd won wouldn't last long.

He glanced toward the cabin and the soft golden light spilling from the windows and onto the porch, and frowned. Warm, welcoming. Home, he thought, his frown deepening. Much more so than his condo near downtown Pueblo had ever felt. The only change he'd made in the exterior of his condo since he'd purchased it several years before was to remove the For Sale sign near the front walk. He'd never thought of the place as home. More as a place to sleep, a place to store his possessions, few as they were.

It was Isabelle, he decided, knowing that she waited inside the cabin for him, reveling in the anticipation that filled him at the mere thought. A man could get used to having a woman waiting for him when he came in from a day's work. Could grow lazy thinking about curling up beside her in bed every night. In two short days, he'd developed a need for her. An addiction that wasn't going to fade easily once they left the cabin and returned to town.

But they couldn't stay here forever, he reminded himself as he stared at the windows, his mind filled with thoughts of her. Somehow he had to find a way to help Isabelle remember the men's names behind the voices she'd overheard. Without the testimony of those two men, he didn't have a case, the evidence he needed, a prayer of putting Brad behind bars where he belonged.

And when she did remember, he thought, dread filling him at the realization, he wouldn't have an excuse to keep her at the cabin any longer. He wouldn't be able to sleep with her at night, feel the warmth of her body curled against his. He'd never again see her face flushed with passion as he filled her. Never wake to find her sleepy, smiling gaze on his.

He heard the screen door squeak open on its hinges, focused his gaze there as Isabelle stepped into the opening. At the sight of her standing there, waiting for him, a warm smile of welcome on her face, resentment poured through him. Resentment for the gap in their social status. Resentment for the gap in their ages.

Resentment for what his stepbrother had done to her.

"Are you coming inside?" she teased. "Or are you going to stand outside all night?"

He forced his lips upward in a smile. "Depends on what's waiting for me inside," he called out.

She slid a hand up high on the door frame and hitched one hip in a provocative pose. "I made chili for dinner," she said as she toyed coyly with the top button of her blouse. "Or we could skip dinner and go straight to bed."

The button slipped open and he watched her fingers stroke sensually, teasingly, over the skin she'd exposed. The sight wiped his mind clean and filled him with heat. "Are you hungry?" he asked as he strode for the porch.

"Not really. Are you?" she asked, peering up at him hopefully as he stopped in front of her.

"Starving." He dipped his head to nibble at her throat. "For you," he added, and nudged her through the doorway.

# Five

——

"**D**id you hear anything while you were in town?"

Link watched the water and bubbles sluice down Isabelle's spine as she leaned forward to shut off the taps and decided that the bubble bath might not have been such a bad idea after all. The suggestion had been hers, one he'd tried to weasel out of, fearing the ribbing he'd receive if the guys at headquarters ever got wind that he'd willingly soaked in a tub full of bubbles scented with something as sissy-sounding as lavender.

She settled back against his chest and fluffed foaming peaks of bubbles over her breasts, and he decided he didn't give a damn what the guys might think. A bubble bath—one taken with Isabelle—was, bar none, the most entertaining, erotic hour he'd ever spent in a tub.

"Not much," he said, and dropped a hand from the side of the tub to pop a particularly large bubble that had lodged strategically over a breast. She tossed a smile over her shoulder and closed her hand over his, holding it over her breast.

"What's not much?" she asked, and swept a small mountain of bubbles to cover their joined hands.

"They recovered your car," he began, and buried his nose in the curve of her neck and inhaled. "It's in the garage at headquarters," he said, releasing the breath on a sigh. "The chief assigned the case to me with instructions to find you ASAP. In the meantime, your daddy's got everybody on the force chasing their tails trying to find you."

She winced and tipped her head back to look at him. "I should call him," she said guiltily. "He must be worried."

"Too chancy," he said, dropping a kiss on her forehead.

She sighed and dropped her chin, nestling her head comfortably against his chest again. "What about Brad? Did you hear anything about him?"

Link scowled, not liking to hear her speak the man's name. "He's convinced you were abducted."

"Abducted!" she echoed, bolting upright and twisting around to look at him. "Why would he think a thing such as that?"

Link lifted a shoulder and touched a finger to the hollow at the base of her throat. "Easier than admitting that you'd left him standing at the altar."

"Surely no one believes that I've been abducted?"

He lifted a shoulder again, dragging his finger

down her chest and beneath the water's surface. "A wrecked car? A missing bride? It would be easy enough to convince someone an abduction had occurred."

She scowled and twisted back around. "I wasn't abducted," she grumbled peevishly, and flopped back against his chest.

"Yeah, you were," he said, and leaned to nip playfully at her earlobe. "I abducted you and I'm holding you hostage as my sex slave."

She huffed a breath, refusing to be distracted from her anger. "You're *my* sex slave. Remember? I seduced *you.*"

He chuckled and lifted his legs over hers, locking them around her waist. "Yeah, I guess you did."

She smoothed a palm over his thigh and back up, wiping away the bubbles. "Link?" she said after a minute.

"Hmm?" he murmured, lulled by the sensual play of her fingers on his leg.

"Do you think I'm...loose?"

He choked on a laugh. "Hardly."

"No, I'm serious," she said, and unwound his legs from around her so that she could turn and face him. "I don't want you to think that I would sleep with just anyone."

He shook his head, unable to believe that she'd think he'd assume such a thing. He swept from her cheek a tendril that had escaped the knot she'd twisted the hair up into. "No. I don't think you're that kind of woman."

Relieved, she dropped a kiss on his lips. "Thank you."

"You're welcome."

She pushed back from him, making the water churn. "Trade places with me."

"What?" he asked in confusion.

"Trade places." She stood, dripping foamy bubbles from her fingers as she placed a hand on his back and urged him forward. Easing around him, she sank back down into the water behind him and stretched her legs out alongside his. "That's better," she said, sounding pleased.

"I don't know," he said doubtfully, already missing the feel of her body snugged up against his. "I kind of liked things the way they were."

"Oh, you'll like this position, too," she promised, and placed her hands on his shoulders and began to knead.

He groaned as her fingers dug deeply into tensed muscles.

"Does that feel good?" she quizzed, pausing to peer at him over his shoulder.

"Don't stop," he begged pitifully.

She laughed and resumed her massage. "My brothers swear I have magic fingers."

"Wise men, your brothers."

"Yes, they are." She leaned to peer at him again but continued her massage. "Do you have any brothers or sisters?"

He tensed, then forced his muscles to relax. "No." It wasn't a lie, he told himself. He didn't have any full-blood brothers. Only one stepbrother, whom he'd never claimed relationship to, anyway.

"That's sad," she murmured sympathetically. "I can't imagine my life without my brothers." She laughed then and leaned to whisper at his ear. "Promise me you'll never tell them I said that."

He angled his head slightly, frowning. "Why?"

"Because I've spent a great deal of time and effort trying to convince them that they are a royal pain in the you-know-what."

"Why?"

"Because they're too protective." She shifted her legs more comfortably around him and moved her fingers to cup his neck. "It's like having three fathers," she said, kneading at the tendons there. "Bossing me around and checking up on me."

"They do it because they care."

"Yes," she agreed readily. "But it's infuriating having them hover all the time. You can't imagine what it's like to be treated as if you're a glass doll. Protected and guarded as if you'd break at the slightest jarring."

Because he felt the need to treat her similarly, and because he feared he'd never have the chance to do so once they left the cabin, Link remained silent.

"I was never allowed to do anything that other girls my age were allowed to do," she continued. "No overnights. No extracurricular activities. No shopping sprees at the mall. Unless I was accompanied by one of my brothers, of course," she added, then snorted indelicately. "Imagine shopping for personal items with your brothers along. How embarrassing! And

frustrating, too. They were always pressing me to
hurry, rolling their eyes when I'd dare ask their opin-
ion on a particular style or color.'' She chuckled and
leaned close to his ear again. ''Sometimes I would
purposely hold up something really risqué just to
make them blush.''

Link frowned as she began to knead his neck again,
realizing for the first time how truly sheltered her life
must have been. ''What was it like when you were
away?'' he asked curiously. ''Back east at that boarding school and in Europe?''

''The same. Only my brothers weren't there hovering. It was usually some other family member, or a
teacher that my father employed to watch over me.
While in Europe, it was a trusted friend of the family.
I've never truly been on my own. Ever.''

He absorbed that slowly, knowing the reason why.
The kidnapping. Reason enough to want to shelter
her. Protect her.

He caught her hand in his and tugged it down his
chest, drawing her face next to his. ''And what would
you do you if you had the freedom to do anything
you wanted?'' He glanced over at her. ''Anything,''
he repeated.

She frowned slightly, then a smile began to grow,
quickly spreading across her face and lighting her
eyes. ''A fair. I've always wanted to attend a fair.
Ride a roller coaster. Eat cotton candy. Throw balls
at a target and win a bear.'' She laughed and curled
her fingers around his. ''Of course, I'd probably miss
the target, but it would be fun, just the same.''

He pushed himself to his feet, making Isabelle

squeal and grab for the edge of the tub to keep from sliding under the water. Then he turned and reached down, pulling her up, dripping, into his arms. "We'll go to one. Tomorrow," he promised.

She looked up at him, her eyes going round. "A fair? Where?"

He shook his head, wondering if he was risking their location, as well as Isabelle's safety, with his desire to make up to her all she'd lost. "I don't know." Sure that he could find a fair remote enough, one where their appearance wouldn't arouse suspicion, he hugged her to him. Bubbles exploded between their bodies, the beads of moisture tickling their bare flesh. "But I'll find one. If I have to drive you all the way to Texas, I'll find you a fair."

Link didn't have to drive her all the way to Texas. Just across two counties before he located a small fair in a rural area. They arrived just after dusk, with Isabelle wearing an old flannel shirt he'd found in the closet and her face shadowed by a ball cap he'd insisted she wear to further disguise her identity.

Her fingers tightened around his as they walked hand in hand past booth after booth with carnies calling to them to try their luck at the games of chance.

"This is wonderful," she murmured, awed by the sights and sounds that whirled around her.

He glanced down at her and smiled. "You haven't even ridden the first ride, or had the first bite of cotton candy."

"It doesn't matter," she said, giving his hand a grateful squeeze. "Just to be here, to experience all this. It's...awesome. Oh!'' she cried, stumbling to a stop and staring. "A roller coaster. Can we ride it?" she asked, whipping her head around to look up at him, her eyes filled with hope.

He tossed back his head and laughed, then released her hand to sling his arm around her shoulders. "How 'bout we start with something milder, like the Ferris wheel," he suggested, pointing, and turned her in that direction. She stumbled along at his side, her head angled back over her shoulder, watching longingly as the roller coaster chugged to the top of the first rise, then pitched forward, its passengers screaming, some even waving their arms bravely above their heads. "Later," she said, turning to peer up at him. "We can ride it later, can't we?"

He chuckled and hugged her against his side. "Yes, and any other ride that strikes your fancy."

He stood in line and purchased two tickets for the Ferris wheel, then caught her hand again and tugged her to the gate, where the attendant swung a bar open for them and waved them into the swaying bucket that waited. Once they were seated, the attendant snapped the safety bar across their laps, then gave the bucket a push, sending them bouncing on their way.

Wide-eyed, Isabelle tipped back her head, staring up at the star-studded sky as the Ferris wheel ground to a stop to take on another group of passengers. Once loaded, it jerked into motion again, spinning them higher. She leaned forward to look out over the carnival grounds. "Oh, this is marvelous," she cried. "We're up so high!"

"Careful," Link warned when she leaned too far

forward, making the bucket tilt precariously. He locked an arm firmly around her waist and drew her back.

She settled against his side on a sigh, then looked up at him. "When we reach the top, will you kiss me?"

He choked on a laugh. "What?"

"I want you to kiss me at the top," she insisted. "Imagine the thrill. Sitting on top of the world and being kissed senseless." She dropped her hand on his thigh and squeezed. "You will, won't you? Please?"

Completely taken with her childlike excitement, the rosy flush of her cheeks, Link lowered his face over hers. "How about we start now and build?" he suggested. He brushed his lips over hers. Once. Twice. Then wrapped his arms around her and drew her to him. The Ferris wheel jerked to a stop again, making their mouths bump hard, their teeth scrape. They laughed, then found each other's mouths again as the bucket churned higher still. When they reached the top, Isabelle was clinging to him, her heart pounding like a kettledrum against his chest, her lips welded to his.

He slowly tore his mouth from hers as the bucket jerked to a stop, then leaned to peer over the side and down at the ground below. He glanced over at Isabelle and bit back a grin when he found her eyes still closed. "Open your eyes, Isabelle."

She drew in a deep breath, then forced her lids slowly open. Blinked. Blinked again, as if waking from a sweet dream, to peer at him.

"You're on top of the world now," he said softly.

She turned her head slowly, her eyes growing wide with wonder as she took in the sights. The stars twinkling above them, the colorful lights flashing below. People milling around on the ground, some running to catch the next ride, the next thrill. Others simply strolling along, content just to watch. The smells drifting up to them. Spun sugar on paper cones, buttery corn on the cob, the greasy, mouth-watering scent of meat grilling. The sounds. A cacophony of voices, blending with the engines that powered the rides, music blaring scratchily from hidden speakers.

She breathed deeply, absorbing it all, then turned to him. "Kiss me again."

Link lay on his side with Isabelle curled against him, her head nestled in the crook of his arm. He could feel the rhythm and warmth of each breath she drew. In. Out. In. Out. Measured each one in the slow rise and fall of the breast crushed against his chest. His own breathing slowed to match hers as he stared down at her sleeping face, stroking his palm down her cheek, his fingers along her jaw, letting his fingertips drift slowly off her chin. He could feel the soft beat of her heart, thrumming against his. He stilled, listening, as their individual rhythms blended and beat as one.

Smiling tenderly, he laid a hand over her cheek again and smoothed the ball of his thumb across her lips. To say he felt protective of her would be an understatement. To deny he'd fallen in love with her, a lie.

He'd never tire of watching her. Of touching her.

Yet, he knew he had no right to do either of those things. She was a Fortune. A young woman of means, refinement beyond anything he'd ever known or experienced in his thirty-five years. He was an old man compared to her twenty-two years. Older still if he counted experience. And though he suspected she thought herself in love with him, too, he was wise enough to know a relationship with her would end in disaster. She'd been protected most of her life. Guarded. Cushioned. All but smothered.

And now she was spreading her wings a bit. Probably for the first time in her life. And he was simply a part of that rebellion, that heady race to see, touch and experience everything she'd once been shielded from. Not that he'd minded being a part of her rebellion. He'd received more pleasure from their time together, their mating, than she, he was sure.

But it would end soon. It had to. It was his job to see that it did. And when he returned her to her family, when he watched her walk away from him, he knew his heart would break a little. No, he thought, swallowing hard as looked down at her. His heart would split wide open, weep like a festered wound for the rest of his sorry days.

But he wouldn't regret their time together, he promised himself. Given the chance, he wouldn't step back three days and change a single decision he'd made. He still would have made love with her when she'd offered herself to him, and every time since. With her, he'd known joy for the first time in his life. Discovered it first when she'd come apart around him in a climax that had rocked his soul, but no less intense than when he'd watched her eyes light up as she'd stepped from his Blazer and spotted the bright and noisy carnival across the field from where they'd parked.

She was undoubtedly the sexiest, most loving and giving woman he'd ever known.

But he'd take her home, he promised himself. Back to her family, the world she was familiar with, comfortable in. To do anything less would be worse than what his stepbrother had tried to do to her. Steal her away from her family, strip her of her pride, her innocence, and leave her with nothing but haunting memories and regrets.

Isabelle glanced up from the stove and smiled as Link stepped from the bedroom the next morning. "Are you going into Pueblo today?"

He shook his head as he pulled out a chair, then dropped down on it, tossing the guest list onto the table. "No. I figured I could do more good here, helping you go over the list again."

She picked up a cloth, wrapped it around the handle of the coffeepot and crossed to the table. Peering over his shoulder at the pages he flipped through, she smoothed a hand over his hair in an unconscious gesture of affection as she poured him a cup of coffee.

He glanced up at her, then quickly down, and snatched up the cup. "Thanks," he murmured, and gulped a drink. The coffee burned his tongue, seared the roof of his mouth and scorched a path all the way down his throat. But he used the pain to focus his attention back on the task at hand and off Isabelle.

"I've gone over the names at least a hundred times, Link," she complained wearily. "I just can't place the voices with any of the people listed there."

"I thought we'd try something different," he suggested, and picked up a page. "I'll say the names out loud, quiz you about them, and see if that doesn't spark some memory."

She sighed and shoved the coffeepot onto the table, then pressed a hip against his side. He glanced up at her as she squirmed until she'd created enough space for her to slide onto his lap. She wiggled around until she was comfortable—and Link was anything but— then picked up a page and sank back against his chest. "Okay," she said in resignation, and held up a page for him to read. "Quiz away."

It took Link a minute to find his voice. "Wouldn't you be more comfortable in the other chair? Or maybe the sofa?"

She angled her head to peer at him, a slight frown puckered between her brows. "No. Why? Are you uncomfortable?"

He couldn't look at her. Didn't dare. Not when he'd decided it was time to start reestablishing the boundaries of their relationship again. Place them back where they belonged. That of criminal investigator of a murder case protecting a key witness. But it was hard to think along those terms with her sitting on his lap, that firm rear end of hers planted firmly against his sex.

He dragged in a breath. "No. I'm fine."

"Good," she said with a satisfied nod, and turned

her gaze back to the page. "Dr. and Mrs. Stuart Addison."

He shifted her on his lap, giving himself some room. "Who are they?" he asked.

"Friends of my parents. They live in Boston."

"Can you picture him?"

"Yes. Short, fat and bald. And Mrs. Addison looks just like him."

In spite of his discomfort, Link found himself laughing. "You're making that up."

"I'm not! Though she does wear a wig when she's in public," she added prudently.

He shook his head and slapped the back of his hand against the page. "Who's next?"

"Arthur Ashworth."

"And?" he prodded.

She pursed her lips, puzzling over the name. "I think he's an author. Writes legal thrillers." She shook her head and glanced down at the list again, frowning. "But I could be wrong."

"Arthur Ashworth the Author. Triple A." Link shook his head again. "This could get comical."

"If you think that's bad," she said, flipping pages, "wait until you hear this one." She found the name she wanted and read, "Welton Presley Peters. How's that for a name?"

"Sounds like one of those tongue-twisters we used to say when we were kids."

"He's a college fraternity brother of my father's. One my mother detested," she added, then sputtered a laugh. "If you think his name is bad, you should hear his nickname."

Unable to resist, Link asked, "What is it?"

"Well-Pressed. He was fastidious about his appearance, or so I'm told. But I heard my mother once refer to him by a different nickname. Prissy Prick. Prick being another name for—"

"I get the picture," he said dryly, then nodded toward the list. "What's the next name on the list?"

Disappointed that she hadn't been able to distract him from the list, she shifted on his lap and flipped back to the first page. "Richard Anton. He's the comptroller for Dad's company."

"What does his voice sound like?"

She dipped her chin and pushed out her lips, dropping her voice low. "Like this," she croaked.

Link rolled his eyes. "Come on, Issie. Get serious. We've got a lot of names to cover."

She tossed the papers to the table in frustration. "It's a waste of time. I've gone over this list again and again, and not one of the names hits a nerve." She dragged a finger beneath her nose and sniffed, making him glance her way.

He brushed her hair back from her cheek. "Hey," he said softly, when he saw that tears swam in her eyes. "I didn't mean to upset you."

"It's not you," she said, sniffing again. "It's *that*," she said, gesturing angrily at the list. "I'm just sick of thinking about it all."

"Then don't," he soothed, turning her across his lap and drawing her against his chest. "You're probably just trying too hard."

She buried her face in the curve of his neck. "I want it to be over," she said tearfully.

Which was exactly what Link wanted, too, but when it was, when Brad was behind bars, and he and Isabelle no longer had a reason to remain at the cabin...

Link stopped the thought before it could fully form. He wouldn't think about what would happen then, he told himself. He'd just think about now.

He pressed his lips against her hair and inhaled deeply, drawing in her scent. A scent that drew memories of a bubble bath shared together, a long ride on a Ferris wheel. "Don't cry," he murmured. "It'll be over soon enough."

"But I—"

Hearing a sound, he tightened his arms around her, shushing her, and lifted his head, listening.

"What?" she asked, raising her head. "Did you hear something?"

He pressed a finger against her lips and stood, shifting her onto the chair as he rose. Keeping out of sight of the front window, he eased to its side. He lifted a corner of the drape and peered cautiously out.

"What is it?" she whispered anxiously. "Is someone coming?"

He nodded but kept his gaze on the dirt road that led to the cabin, listening as the sound of the engine grew louder. He saw the front bumper appear first, bouncing into view over the rise, then the rest of the vehicle appeared.

"What the hell," he muttered in surprise, and stepped boldly in front of the window to stare.

Isabelle popped up from the chair and hurried to his side, leaning to peer around him. "Who is it?"

"Hank," he said, unable to believe what he was seeing. "My partner." Then he swore and headed for the door. "I'll kill the son of a bitch," he muttered under his breath, "if he's blown our cover."

Isabelle hurried after him, stepping out onto the porch behind him just as the battered Jeep screeched to a stop in front of the cabin.

Hank was climbing out of the driver's side, his hands up in the air as if in surrender, as he looked up at Link. "I swear this isn't my fault," he was saying as the passenger door opened on the opposite side of the Jeep and a man in a suit stepped out.

Isabelle's eyes widened in dismay. "Daddy?" she whispered in disbelief as she stepped around Link to stare.

Hunter Fortune rounded the front of the Jeep, his face mottled, his finger leveled accusingly at Link. "I'll have your badge for this," he growled. "You'll be *damn* lucky if I don't have your life for kidnapping my daughter."

Isabelle stepped quickly in front of Link as if to protect him. "No, Daddy," she said, shaking her head wildly. "Link didn't kidnap me. He rescued me, then brought me here to keep me safe."

"Safe from *whom?*" her father shouted. "From your family who loves you? From the man who loves you, the one you were supposed to marry?" He swiped an arm through the air in front of his chest. "Get away from him, Isabelle."

She took a step back, her hips bumping against Link's groin, and reached behind her, placing her hands on the sides of his thighs. "No. You don't understand. Link is—"

"Nothing but a lowlife who let the power behind the badge go to his head. A badge he'd never have received if I'd known his history. Now, get away from him. And you," he said, spinning to level a finger at Hank, "do your job. Arrest him."

Hank turned a pitying look on Link. "Sorry, buddy," he said regretfully. "I swear I didn't tell him anything. He came to me and demanded that I bring him here. Grilled me the entire trip. I swear I didn't tell him anything about your past. Seems he's done some detective work of his own. I thought it best to do as he asked and bring him here and let you explain it all to him."

Frustrated by the confusing conversation that was going on around her, Isabelle stamped her foot. "Stop it!" she cried. "Stop it right this instant! No one is going to arrest Link. He hasn't done anything but protect me from a murderer."

"Isabelle," Link warned in a low voice.

"Well, it's true," she cried, whirling to face him. "You rescued me from my car and brought me here to keep me safe from Brad."

"Brad!" her father roared behind her. "You don't need protecting from Brad! You need protecting from him!" he shouted, jabbing a finger at Link again.

"Maybe if we all just went inside and talked this over calmly," Hank suggested mildly.

"Oh, we're going to talk, all right," Hunter Fortune grated as he marched for the porch. "And this man," he said with a nod of his head toward Link as he passed him, "had better have some damn good answers for the questions I have for him."

He jerked open the door, then stepped back, lifting his chin imperiously as he waited for the others to file inside before him. Hank passed by first, his hands shoved deeply into his pockets. He lifted a shoulder as if to say "don't ask me" as he brushed past Isabelle and Link.

When Isabelle hesitated, her father narrowed an eye at her. "Isabelle," he said, his voice sharp with warning.

Shooting her father a furious look, Isabelle snatched Link's hand and, with a stubborn lift of her chin, strode past her father, tugging Link behind her.

Snarling under his breath at her open defiance, her father followed, letting the door slam behind him.

"Sit," Hunter ordered.

Isabelle folded her arms beneath her breasts and tipped her chin higher. "You're forgetting your manners, Dad. This isn't your home."

"Nor is it yours," he growled.

"It's mine," Hank said helpfully, and dragged a chair from the kitchen to place beside Hunter. He patted the seat. "Here you go, Mr. Fortune. Have a seat."

His nostrils flaring in barely controlled fury, Hunter gave his slacks a hitch at the knee, then sank down, his spine ramrod straight. He waited silently, pointedly, while Isabelle and Link moved to sit on the sofa, and Hank dropped down on the sofa's arm.

"So," Hank said cheerfully, slapping his hands

down on his knees as he glanced around the room at everyone. "Can I offer anyone anything to drink?"

Link moaned and dropped his forehead onto his palms and his elbows onto his knees.

"No, thank you," Isabelle said politely, then glanced at her father. "Dad?"

"No," he barked, then squirmed in his chair when she pursed her lips at him in disapproval. He folded his arms across his chest, his face reddening, but muttered the appropriate niceties under his breath.

"Well!" Hank said, giving his knees another slap. "If no one's thirsty, I guess that leaves us with nothing to do but discuss what we came inside to talk about."

# Six

———

"**B**rad killed Mike Dodd."

At Isabelle's blunt pronouncement, Link groaned against his hands, while her father leaped up from his chair. Fortune's chest puffed to the point where he looked as if he might burst his shirt's buttons at any minute, or float to the ceiling like a helium-filled balloon.

"Isabelle!" he roared. "What has come over you?"

She met his gaze defiantly. "It's true. Brad killed Mike Dodd."

"It's him," Hunter accused, pointing a finger at Link again. "He's filled your head with this nonsense to hide his own guilt."

Before Link had a chance to respond, to share the evidence he'd gathered that pointed to Brad's guilt,

Isabelle snapped, "Link is guilty of nothing but trying to see justice served. I know Brad's guilty because I overheard two men talking just before the wedding, and they alluded to Brad's part in Mike's death."

"Who?" her father demanded to know. "Name them and I'll drag them before the grand jury myself."

Isabelle dropped her gaze and plucked at the skirt of her dress. "I don't know," she murmured.

Hunter's expression turned smug. "Just as I thought. You're trying to protect him, aren't you?" He glanced around the small room, the solitary bedroom and unmade bed beyond the single interior door in plain view, then narrowed his eyes on the top of Link's bowed head. "And just exactly *what* has been going on in this cabin while the two of you have been hiding out here?"

Link jerked up his head at the insinuation to glare at Hunter, then turned to level a look on Hank. Hank received the silent message and rose. "Isabelle," he said, offering her his hand. "Why don't you and I take a little walk?"

"B-but—" she stammered. Hank caught her hand and pulled her to her feet.

"Go," Link ordered under his breath when she continued to hesitate. "I can handle this."

With a last worried look at Link, then a quelling look at her father, Isabelle allowed Hank to lead her from the cabin.

Once they were gone, Link rose to glare down at Fortune. "I don't care what you think about me," he said tersely, "or what you think you *know* about me, but my main concern throughout all of this has been Isabelle's safety and well-being.''

"As has been mine," her father replied furiously.

"Fine," Link snapped. "Then we don't have a problem."

"Oh, but we do. Starting with the lies about Brad you've filled Isabelle's head with.''

"They aren't lies!" Link shouted, then slapped a hand against the back of his neck and turned away, kneading at the tension there. "What Isabelle told you is the truth," he said, struggling for calm as he began to pace. "Just before the wedding was scheduled to begin, she overheard two men talking in the vestibule of the church. What they said convinced her that Brad murdered Mike Dodd. She was frightened. Unsure what to do. So she ran.''

"She could have come to me with her concerns.''

Link whirled, his face red with rage. "There wasn't time, dammit! There were only minutes before the wedding was to begin. She panicked and she ran. And I don't blame her," he added furiously. "She was running for her life.''

Hunter's face paled at the desperate image Link painted for him and sank weakly down to the chair. "I would have protected her. I would never let anyone harm her again.''

"Wouldn't you?" Link asked, taking a step closer. "You *expected* her to marry Brad Rowan. Her words, not mine," he added when Hunter lifted his head to glare at him. "She didn't love Brad. She only agreed to marry him to please you. All of you. To give her family that piece of land. To repay you for all you've sacrificed for her."

"No," Hunter said, wagging his head in denial. "Isabelle's happiness, her well-being, is much more important to me, us, than any piece of land."

"Obviously, she didn't think so, because she was willing to sacrifice both for a piece of real estate."

Hunter closed his hands over his knees and gripped them, rocking back and forth as he stared unseeing at the sofa where his daughter had sat only moments before. "She doesn't understand the ways of the world," he said, suddenly looking old, beaten. "We've protected her. Shielded her from unpleasantries."

"Smothered her," Link muttered.

Hunter snapped up his head. "Because of what happened to her," he said, his voice thick with accusation. "The abduction," he added, rising. "Which you know the details of all too well, don't you?"

The allegation hit its mark, a direct strike to Link's heart, his very soul, making him collapse inward, as if he'd taken a slug from a .38 in the chest. "Yes," he moaned, and turned away. "But I had nothing to do with it."

"But you were privy to it. You knew your stepbrother had taken her. You had to have known. You lived in the same house with him."

Link straightened and inhaled deeply, trying to ease the pain in his chest. In his heart. Seeing again the news footage of Isabelle's face as she'd been carried from the cabin by the SWAT team. "How did you find out?" he whispered.

"Public records, for the most part," Fortune told him. "Everybody's included in them, whether they are privy to the fact, or not. When you arrested Riley, I was furious. I knew you had the wrong man, yet you seemed determined to blame my son for a crime he didn't commit. I wanted to find out everything I could about you. Prove your ineptness, destroy your credibility so that the authorities would be forced to release Riley. But then *you* released him, before my own investigation of you was complete.

"My interest in you should have waned then," he continued, "but it didn't. It only increased. Why would you arrest Riley, then work diligently to prove his innocence? I asked myself this same question over and over again, without finding an acceptable answer." He shook his head, as if even now he didn't understand Link's actions.

"I studied every piece of information about you that I could get my hands on," he said, continuing. "From your birth records on. Nothing. I could find nothing to fault you with. A man who had lived an impoverished life, dragged around by a mother who married again and again, each time seemingly more foolishly. A man who graduated from high school with exemplary grades, in spite of never remaining in the same school system for more than six months. A man who went on to college where he worked his way through to a degree in criminal justice over a period of seven years."

He shook his head again as he continued to study Link. "I could find nothing to fault you with," he repeated. "Until I happened to notice your mother's last name. The name she carried at the time of Isabelle's abduction.''

"Razley," Link muttered bitterly.

"Yes, Razley," Fortune confirmed. "I knew then that you, more than likely, were aware of Isabelle's abduction. Suspected that you might even have been involved."

"Yes, I knew," Link murmured, fighting back the guilt that the admission, the association, drew. "But I wasn't involved. And I didn't know where they held her."

"Then why did you remain silent? Why didn't you tell the police what you knew?"

Link whirled, his face red, his body stiff with rage. "I couldn't come forward until I knew where they held her. The media were all over the place. Someone in the department could have leaked them the story, revealing the kidnappers' identity. If they had, my stepbrother Joe and his accomplice would have killed her. I know they would."

Fortune's eyes sharpened, then narrowed suspiciously. "You made the call, didn't you? You were the one who told the police where to find her."

Link dug his fingers through his hair. "Yes," he moaned, the memory, the fear of what Joe would do to her, might already have done to her, filling him again.

"But you refused to reveal your name, to collect the reward we offered."

Link dropped his hands and turned away with an angry snarl. "I didn't want your money."

"Then what did you want? What did you expect

to gain by exposing your stepbrother's guilt and that of his friend when you made that call?''

"Nothing." Link felt the emotion swelling in his chest, burning in his throat. He tipped his head back and gulped it back. "I just wanted them to let her go. She was just a little girl. Innocent. I wanted her home. With her family. Where she belonged."

"They would have killed her. They planned to, you know."

Link groaned, squeezing his eyes shut against the reality of that, wishing that Fortune would stop pounding him with the reminders, with all the fears he'd lived with those three days. "I knew what they were capable of."

"They'd hurt you before, hadn't they? That's what earned you the scars on your face. Joe Razley was mean to the bone and enjoyed abusing you. I found the emergency room records where you were treated for a laceration on your face. He did that to you, yet you refused to name him for fear the police would arrest him."

Link could only nod, unable to push a sound past the emotion that still clotted in his throat, remembering his fear for his mother, fear of what Joe or his old man would do to Link's mother if Link had dared squeal on his stepbrother. They had both lived in fear of the Razley men since his mother's marriage to Joe, Sr. when Link was nine years old.

"And knowing that, knowing that if you stepped forward and exposed them, you were endangering your own life, you made that call, informing the police of Isabelle's whereabouts."

Link clenched his teeth. "Yes," he ground out. "I knew what they were capable of. What they would do to her. Was haunted by what they might have already done."

He felt a hand close over his shoulder, the dig of fingers squeezing deep. A shudder quaked through him, but he stiffened his spine, refusing to give into the emotion.

"And you'll keep her safe now," Hunter said quietly. "I'm entrusting her care to you. Make damn sure that you earn that trust."

Isabelle stood on the dirt road and watched the Jeep drive away. She wasn't sure what had happened after she and Hank had left the cabin, what all had transpired between her father and Link. She only knew that when she and Hank had returned from their walk, her father had been waiting by the Jeep and Link was nowhere in sight. Her father had given Isabelle a tight hug, waved Hank behind the wheel, then climbed inside. They'd driven away without her father saying a word to her.

She glanced toward the cabin, her stomach knotted in dread, then raced toward the porch and up the steps.

"Link?" she called as she pulled open the door and stepped inside. She stopped, her heart seeming to stop, too, when she saw him standing in the kitchen, his hands braced on the edge of the sink, staring out the window. She gulped a breath at the rigidness of his spine, the hard set of his jaw, then crossed to him and placed a hand on his back. Leaning around him to peer up at him, she said, "Link? Are you okay?"

She felt a shudder move through him before he turned. "Yeah. I'm fine."

But he wasn't fine. She could see that. Something had changed. "What happened?" she asked, the dread winding tighter at the lack of emotion on his face, in his eyes. "What did my father say to you?"

"We just cleared the air a bit, that's all." He stepped around her and moved into the main room. "We've come up with a plan," he said, and picked up the chair Hank had dragged into the room for her father to sit on. He returned it to the kitchen, pushed it beneath the table, then turned away again, avoiding her gaze.

"Plan?" she repeated, staring at him. "What plan?"

"The dedication is tomorrow. The one for the Children's Hospital your family built."

She frantically searched her mind, trying to see the association. "What does that have to do with you? Us?"

"We're going."

Her heart slammed hard against her ribs at the thought of returning to Pueblo, of having to face all those people again. Specifically Brad. "We are?"

"Yes. And you're going to work the crowd," he told her. "I'll stick by your side," he added, as if sensing her fear. "But your job is to listen to voices. See if you can pick up on those of the two men you overheard talking in the sanctuary. Once you nail them, all you have to do is give me a nod, and I'll take it from there."

She gulped. Swallowed hard. "What about Brad? Will he be there?"

He turned to peer at her, his eyes veiled, hiding from her whatever emotion might have been there. "Naturally. He was one of the suppliers your father's company used for materials. Everyone associated with the building of the hospital will be present for the dedication."

Panic winged through her at the thought of seeing Brad again. "But what will I say to him? Do?"

He looked at her, yet through her, never really meeting her gaze. She felt nothing, not even a smidgen of warmth, of compassion from him.

"Nothing," he said, and turned for the bedroom. "You don't have to say or do anything. Ignore him, if you want. You don't owe him anything. Not even an explanation, if you choose not to offer him one."

Isabelle stared after Link, unable to speak, move. What had happened? she asked herself as her knees grew weak. What had her father said to Link that had filled him with this cool disregard for her? What had he done that had turned Link into a total stranger to her?

Isabelle lay in bed, waiting for Link to finish with his shower, her nerves tuned to every sound beyond the closed door. The groan of the pipes when he turned on the water. The wet splat of his bare feet when he stepped into the tub and beneath the spray. The scrape of the metal rings as he jerked the shower curtain along the rod, closing it around him. The gurgle of soapy water emptying down the drain as he rinsed the lather from his body.

She held her breath when the water shut off. Released it slowly as she listened to his feet slap wetly against the floor. She closed her eyes, imagining him drying off...and prayed that when he climbed into bed with her, he would take her in his arms, hold her, make love to her. Then she'd know that everything was all right. That nothing had changed between them.

She heard the door squeak open on its hinges, but kept her eyes closed, not wanting him to see the fear there. She listened to the pad of his bare feet as he passed by the bed.

Tears burned beneath her closed lids as his footsteps continued, carrying him into the main room. She listened to the squeak of springs as he sat down on the sofa. The click of the light switch, signifying that he was sleeping on the sofa and not with her. Drawing in a ragged breath, she buried her face against the pillow.

Oh, God, she moaned silently, feeling her heart breaking. What had she done? What had her *father* done or said that had changed things? She'd been so sure of Link's feelings for her, hers for him. They'd been so happy.

What had happened to change all of that?

After several hours of tossing and turning, Isabelle rolled from the bed and to her feet, her chest heaving with anger, her hands fisted at her sides, ready to do battle. She wasn't going to just sit back and let things happen to her any longer, she told herself. Allow people to manipulate her emotions, her actions, her life. She had a right to know what her father had said to Link. And he'd said something, threatened Link in some way, she was sure. There was no other explanation for the sudden change in Link's attitude toward her.

Before her father's arrival, everything had been fine between them. More than fine, she corrected herself, marching for the door. Marvelous. Extraordinary. Off the charts, hedonistically, satisfyingly perfect.

She strode straight for the sofa and stopped, folding her arms beneath her breasts as she glared down at Link's sleeping form. Furious that he could sleep, when she was drowning in uncertainty, miserable because she didn't know what had gone wrong, she lifted a foot and gave his leg a sound kick.

He jackknifed to a sitting position and twisted around, one arm reared back, hand fisted, ready to deliver a punch.

"Hit me," she said, squaring her shoulders, preparing for it. "Go ahead and hit me. At least it would be a sign that you feel something for me, if only anger."

He shook his head as if to clear it, focused on her, then slowly swung his legs over the side of the sofa and dropped his face onto his hands, moaning. "What are you doing up?"

"I couldn't sleep. And it makes me really angry to know that you could."

He dragged his hands down his face and swung his

legs back up on the sofa, pulling the sheet back over himself. "Go back to bed," he grumbled. "We've got a big day ahead of us tomorrow."

Furious that he thought he could tell her what to do, that he could wave her off to bed as if she were a disobedient child, she lifted her foot and kicked him again.

He caught it in his hand this time, throwing her off balance and making her hop to keep from tumbling to the floor.

"What the hell do you think you're doing?" he growled.

"Kicking you. Now, let go of my foot so that I can kick you again."

"Do I look that stupid?"

"I don't know," she replied with a sniff. "It's dark, and I can't see your face."

He released her foot and gave it a shove, sending her stumbling backward several steps before she was able to regain her balance.

He rolled to his side, his back to her, and jerked the sheet up over his shoulder. "Go to bed," he muttered.

"You can't tell me what to do," she cried indignantly.

"I just did."

"Well, I'm not going."

"Fine. But shut the hell up. I'm trying to sleep."

She dropped her jaw, sucking in an outraged breath, then snapped it closed again with a click. "I will *not* shut up. And you can't make me."

He inhaled deeply, audibly, then rolled to his back and narrowed an eye at her. "Wanna bet?"

Seething, she hugged her arms beneath her breasts and jerked up her chin. "Just try it, tough guy, and see what happens."

Their gazes locked and held. Slowly, Link rolled to a sitting position, then to his feet, dropping the sheet as he stood.

Isabelle flicked her gaze down, her eyes widening when she saw that he was nude, then shot her gaze back to his face. She gulped. Swallowed. And tried to remember why she was angry with him.

"I don't want to have to do this, Isabelle," he said with regret. "But I will, if you force me."

She blinked, unsure what he was referring to. "D-do wh-what?"

"Fight you."

She sputtered a nervous laugh. "Fight me?"

"That is what you intended, wasn't it, when you told me that I couldn't make you be quiet?"

"Well, no. I mean, yes!"

He took a step toward her and she took one in retreat.

When he took another threatening step, she pushed out a hand and braced it against his chest, stopping him. "Link, this is ridiculous."

"Yeah. I thought so, too. But you kept pushing, so here we are."

"I merely wanted you to talk to me."

"But I didn't want to talk, remember? I wanted to sleep."

"Well, you could have slept, and without interruption, if only you had talked to me earlier this evening.''

He rolled his eyes. ''You're not making a lick of sense.''

''I'm not making any sense!'' she cried, insulted. ''And what about you? You have your friend Hank take me for a walk and when I return I'm greeted by a stranger.''

Scowling, he shoved her hand from his chest. ''I'm going to bed.''

''No, you most certainly are not!'' she cried, and grabbed his arm, jerking him back around to face her. That she could accomplish that feat—even if she'd only been able to do so because she'd caught Link off guard—surprised her...but it didn't lessen her pleasure any. She snatched her hand from his arm and tucked it beneath her breasts again. ''You're going to tell me what transpired between you and my father this afternoon.''

''I told you. We cleared the air and made plans for tomorrow. End of story.''

''Something happened,'' she argued stubbornly. ''Or something was said. I know, because you're acting differently toward me than you were before my father arrived.''

His eyes narrowed to slits. ''What is it you want, Isabelle? Another toss in the hay?'' He took a step toward her. ''One last tussle between the sheets before you go back to your royal castle in Pueblo?''

Her blood chilled at his tone, at his total disregard for what they'd shared, something that had meant so very much to her. She pushed her hands out, bracing them against his chest. "No," she whispered, fighting to keep her voice from breaking.

He hooked his hands low on her hips and drew her up hard against him. "Are you sure?" He dipped his head to nip at her lower lip. "I'd be more than happy to oblige."

She curled her fingers against his chest, her nails digging deep. She wanted to push him away, to rail at him for taking something so special and making it sound so sordid. For taking her heart and ripping it to shreds. But before she could, he crushed his mouth over hers. Even then, she struggled against him, shoving against his chest, clamping her lips together and refusing to respond to his kiss.

But then he moaned low in his throat, his fingers at her hips relaxing, his lips softening, and he lifted his arms to wrap them around her. A hand cupped the back of her neck, and he angled his face, sipping at her mouth, teasing her lips apart with slow, tender, loving strokes of his tongue.

And she was lost.

Hands that had dug into his chest, determined to push him away, opened, palms stroking high, circling his neck. She rose to her toes to meet his kisses, demand more. When he stooped to catch her behind the knees and swing her up into his arms, she melted against his chest.

And when he carried her to the bed they'd shared, the one where she'd willingly and freely given to him her virginity, she clung to him, drawing him with her as he lowered her down. She opened her arms to him, her body…her heart.

And when he filled her, groaned her name against her lips, tears of joy filled her eyes. "I love you, Link," she whispered.

She felt him stiffen, heard his low moan, and opened her eyes as he lifted his head to peer down at her.

"Don't," he said, his voice husky, his face ravaged by an emotion she couldn't name.

"Don't?"

He pushed himself away from her and twisted around to sit on the side of the bed, his back to her. "Don't love me."

She pressed a hand over her heart, sure that she could hear it breaking.

He rose, rubbing a hand over the back of his neck, a habit that she'd learned over the last few days indicated a high level of frustration. In the past, she might have backed away, not wanting to upset him further, cause him distress. But if she'd learned nothing else since leaving the church four days before, she'd learned that she was entitled to a few emotions of her own.

She pushed herself to a sitting position and snatched the sheet up, covering her nudity. "Sorry," she snapped angrily, "but I don't have that much control over my emotions."

He whirled to glare at her. "It's a mistake. Was from the very beginning. I should never have slept with you."

"A little late for regrets, wouldn't you say?" she replied peevishly.

He dragged in a breath, held it, his body quivering,

then he forced the breath out slowly, his shoulders sagging in defeat. "I never meant to hurt you."

"Oh, please," she said, and folded her arms beneath her breasts as she turned her face away. "I don't want or need your pity."

"I don't pity you. I've never pitied you. I couldn't."

She whipped her head around to glare at him. "Then what *do* you feel for me? Was it all just sex for you? A way to pass the time while you were forced to stay here with me?"

"No one forced me to stay."

"Then why did you?" she cried.

"Because...because I care for you."

She willed herself not to cry. "Please don't attempt to placate me. I'm a big girl. I can handle rejection."

"Dammit, Isabelle!" he shouted. "I'm not trying to placate you, and I'm not rejecting you."

She braced a hand against the tangled covers and leaned toward him, clutching the sheet at her breasts. "What do you call it, if not rejection? I told you that I loved you, I offered you my heart and you tossed it back in my face. If that isn't rejection, then I'd like to know what is."

"Well, if it is, then I'm doing it out of love, not because I want to hurt you."

She stilled, her heart seeming to stop, too. Then she shook her head, inching back on the bed and away from him. "No. You don't love me. You couldn't."

"And why not?" he shouted. "Do you think you have a monopoly on the emotion? Do you think I would have slept with you, taken your virginity, if I didn't feel at least something for you?'' He sucked in a breath through his teeth. ''Well, you're wrong,'' he growled, before she could answer. ''I do love you. But I also know that having a relationship with you outside of this cabin is impossible. It would be insane to even try.''

She stared at him, unable to believe what she'd heard. He loved her? He really loved her? Oh, God, he loved her! ''Why?'' she whispered. ''If you love me, then why can't we be together? Why does it have to end here?''

''Because it does!'' he railed. He tossed a hand at her, gesturing wildly. ''You're Isabelle Fortune and I'm nobody. You've lived with wealth and privilege all your life, while I've lived in the gutter. I can't give you the lifestyle you're accustomed to. I wouldn't know how, even if I had the means.''

She curled her fingers tighter into the sheet. ''You're wrong, Link,'' she said, desperate to make him understand, her body trembling with it. ''The money means nothing to me. It never has. It's you I want. You.''

He dug his fingers through his hair, squeezed at his temples, groaning his frustration, then dropped his hands to his sides. ''You think you do,'' he said wearily. ''And maybe right now that is all you want. But it wouldn't be long before you would begin to resent me, grow to hate me because of all you'd given up, lost because of me.''

She shook her head. ''No, Link. I wouldn't. I could never hate you.''

She watched his face harden, his eyes grow cold.

"Couldn't you?" he asked, and took a step toward the bed. He stopped at its side and leaned forward, bracing his hands against the mattress as he shoved his face close to hers. "Remember the man who kidnapped you? The one who dragged you into the van?"

She shrank away from him, shaking her head. "Don't, Link. You're frightening me."

"Good. You need to be scared. Of me. Of men like me. That man was my stepbrother, Isabelle. My stepbrother," he repeated, letting that revelation soak in. "I knew that he'd kidnapped you. He told me. Called me on the phone and bragged about how he had snatched Hunter Fortune's daughter right off the street. Easy money, he said. Fortune would pay big bucks to get his little girl back. And he wanted to cut me in on the action."

She shook her head wildly, inching farther away. "No," she sobbed. "No!"

"Yes, Isabelle. Yes. He would make the call, demanding the ransom, then set up a place for your father to drop off the cash. A million bucks, Isabelle. A million bucks. More money than I'd ever seen in my life, or probably ever would. And all I had to do for my part was pick up the money from the drop-off point and deliver it to my stepbrother."

Link could see the fear in her eyes, almost smell it. And he could see the revulsion, as well. Saddened by it, but satisfied that he'd accomplished all he'd set out to do, he pushed himself from the bed and straightened, never once moving his gaze from hers. "Couldn't hate me, huh?" he said bitterly. "Seems you lied, Isabelle. You lied."

# Seven

It couldn't be true, she told herself. Link couldn't possibly have been involved in her kidnapping. Isabelle sat stiffly in the passenger seat, her hands fisted tightly on her lap, her eyes riveted on the road ahead. Even if it truly was his stepbrother who had plucked her from the street, Link couldn't have had a part in the kidnapping plot. He just couldn't. Link wasn't that kind of man.

The men who had captured her were mean. Evil. And Link wasn't. He was kind and gentle and tender. When he'd brought her to the cabin after she'd wrecked her car in the desert, he'd done so because she'd asked him to, begged him, even. And he'd never once, throughout their four days at the cabin, tried to take advantage of her. Not physically. Not sexually. It was she who had seduced him. All but forced him to make love to her.

Oh, God, she thought, feeling the tears push at her throat. She loved him. In spite of the things he'd told her, she still loved him. And she didn't believe him. Refused to believe him. He would never have been a part of a plot to harm anyone. Not Link. He'd been nothing but kind to her. Throughout their time in the cabin, his focus had been to protect her.

"I won't let Brad near you."

She flinched at the sound of his voice, then closed her eyes and forced herself to swallow. Slowly she turned to look at him. His eyes were narrowed on the road, his lips set in a hard, thin line, his hands gripped tightly around the steering wheel. A vein pulsed at his neck. Another at his temple. Was he angry with her? Or just focused on his job and what awaited them at the dedication?

And when it was over, she thought, feeling the panic rising, what then? Would she never she him again? Would they go their separate ways?

Unable to bear the thought of losing him, she reached to touch a hand to his sleeve. "Link—"

He shook free, ignoring the entreaty in her voice. "There'll be a lot of people there," he said, with a nod at the road ahead. "But you don't have anything to worry about. Hank'll be there, as well as most of the other guys on the force. And I'll stick close to your side. Nobody will harm you. You have my word on that. No one will get close enough to lay a hand on you."

But *he'd* hurt her, she thought, her heart stinging

with it. She tore her gaze from the hard set of his jaw and turned to stare through the windshield at the hospital that loomed in the distance.

She couldn't imagine anything or anyone hurting her more than Link had with his rejection.

Hunter Fortune strode straight for Isabelle and Link as they entered the reception area, as if he'd been watching for their arrival.

"Isabelle," her father murmured, drawing her against his chest in an emotional hug. "Are you okay?"

"Just play it cool," Link warned under his breath, glancing around. "You don't want to draw any more attention to her than necessary."

"Of course," Hunter said, and released Isabelle to catch her hand in his. He gave her a confident smile. "We'll get through this, sweetheart," he said, and gave her hand a reassuring squeeze. "And when this is over—"

"Have you seen Rowan?"

Hunter glanced Link's way at the interruption, barely able to contain the snarl that the mention of Brad's name drew. "Not yet. And if he's smart, he won't show his face here."

"Oh, he'll show," Link offered wryly. "His arrogance won't allow him to stay away." His fingers on Isabelle's elbow dug a little deeper. "I need to check in with Hank," he said, his gaze on her father. "Can you keep an eye on Isabelle for a minute?"

Fortune stepped forward, his smile sympathetic as he wrapped an arm around Isabelle's waist. "Of course. We'll be in the administrator's office. You can meet us there when you're done."

Isabelle felt the pressure of Link's fingers on her elbow increase before he released her and her father led her away. But she didn't look at him. She couldn't. She was afraid if she did, she would give in to the tears she kept stubbornly at bay.

As she stepped into the office, she turned to face her father. "What did you say to Link?"

Her father arched a brow, obviously as startled by the abruptness of her question as he was by the anger in her voice. "When?"

"Yesterday. At the cabin."

He lifted a shoulder. "We discussed the plans for today."

"What else?" she demanded, her voice rising shrilly. "I know there was something else said."

"Isabelle," he said, his tone patronizing as he stepped toward her. "There's no need for you to upset yourself over—"

She stepped back. "No," she warned, putting out a hand to stop him. "I will not be placated or protected any longer. I want the truth, and I want to hear it now."

Her father stopped, a slight frown knitting his brow as he peered closely at her. "My God," he murmured, his eyebrows shooting high as he took a step back. "You're in love with him."

She jerked up her chin. "Yes. And I was sure that he loved me, too, until yesterday afternoon. Something happened. Something changed him. And I want to know what that was.''

''If you're thinking that I instructed him to stay away from you, you're wrong. Just the opposite, in fact. I told him that I was entrusting him with your care.''

Tears filled her eyes and she pressed a hand over her eyes to force them back. Duty. Link considered the job of protecting her his duty and would have fulfilled the obligation whether ordered to by her father, or not. He considered it his job to protect her. And he was a man who placed duty above all else. Even his own safety.

*A lowlife who let the power behind the badge go to his head. A badge he'd never have received if I'd known his history.*

She reeled dizzily as the words her father had shouted at Link the afternoon before shot into her mind, numbing her.

''You knew that Link's stepbrother was one of my kidnappers, didn't you?'' she whispered, her gaze locked on her father's face as the realization dawned. ''That was what you were referring to when you said those spiteful things to him when you first arrived yesterday.''

''Yes,'' he said cautiously. ''But not until recently.''

''Did you discuss that with him? Did you discuss the kidnapping?''

''Yes,'' he replied, and turned away, obviously ashamed of the wrongful assumptions he'd made about Link. "He told me everything. Some things that I didn't know."

"What? What did he tell you?"

"He confirmed what I already knew, what I'd un- earthed in my own investigation of his past." He sighed heavily. "But he also revealed something that I didn't know—that I'd only begun to suspect."

"What?" she cried, desperate to know it all.

He turned his head to look at her over his shoulder. "He made the call. Link was the anonymous caller. The one who informed the police of your where- abouts."

Link had been responsible for her rescue.

Isabelle played that realization over and over in her mind as Link slowly but methodically moved her through the crowd gathered for the dedication. She wanted to confront him with her discovery. Demand that he explain why he'd avoided telling her that part of his involvement in her kidnapping, when he'd seemed so anxious, so determined for her to hear the rest.

But now wasn't the time, she told herself. She needed to focus on her purpose here: to identify the men who could name Brad's culpability in Mike Dodd's death. Later, she promised herself. Later she would demand an explanation from Link. Later she would prove to him that he meant more to her than any material wealth. More than anything or any- one ever had in her life.

But for now, she would focus on the people around

her, their voices, just as he seemed focused on his promise to protect her.

She felt as if her face would shatter from the stiffness of the smile she kept frozen in place. Thankfully, no one had mentioned her disappearance, or questioned her about breaking her engagement with Brad. Breeding, she thought with a silent prayer of gratitude for the manners it demanded. Everyone present was too well-bred to broach the subject in her presence.

But she was certain that didn't keep them from whispering about it—and her—behind her back.

She could feel the weight of their gazes as they speculated about the man at her side. The man whose hand had not once left her elbow since he'd collected her earlier from the hospital administrator's office and her father's care.

She thought she caught a few envious glances from women in the room as they silently appraised her escort. If her mind were not so fixed on listening to the voices that swirled around her, if her nerves weren't so frayed, she might have preened a bit at their envious looks. Without question, she was with the most handsome man in the room. A fact that wasn't lost on her. Beneath a black silk blazer, Link wore a white collarless shirt. Though the jacket was loose-fitting, it didn't hide the width of his shoulders, the breadth of his chest, the muscles that played beneath the jacket with each move he made. Nor did it hide the slight bulge of the gun tucked into the shoulder holster he wore beneath it.

"Templeton."

She shifted her gaze to see Hank bearing down on

them. Though resentful of his part in removing her from the cabin the previous day, she forced her smile to remain in place and extended her hand in greeting. "Hello, Hank. How are you?"

He took her hand, squeezed it between his own, his eyes searching hers as he peered at her intently. "Fine. And you?"

He was worried about her, she thought in surprise. She could see it in his eyes, feel it in the firm grip he held on her hand. That he would be concerned for her touched her heart. She gave his hand a reassuring squeeze. "I'm fine."

She felt Link's frown but refused to look at him. Couldn't. Not and resist throwing herself into his arms and begging him to give their relationship a chance.

Link stepped closer, his body forming a triangle of sorts with theirs.

"Problem?" he asked Hank in a low voice.

Hank glanced over at him, then returned his gaze to Isabelle's. "He's here," he said for their ears only. "Rowan. He just arrived."

The blood drained from Isabelle's face, leaving her feeling weak-kneed, helpless, exposed. She slicked her lips. "Where?" she whispered, and glanced covertly around.

Link tightened his grip on her elbow, his fingers digging deep. "Don't look," he ordered in a clipped voice. "Avoid making eye contact, if at all possible."

She dropped her gaze to the hand still grasped tightly within Hank's and slowly redrew it. "It'll be impossible to avoid him if he approaches me. What will I say to him if he does?''

"He won't dare come near you," Link muttered fiercely. "Not as long as I'm with you."

Isabelle looked at him then. Saw the cold fury in his eyes, the determined set of his jaw. And her love for him grew, as did her concern. "I don't want you hurt," she said, her voice trembling at the thought. "Not because of me."

His eyes held hers, burned into her soul, before he tore his gaze away. "Risk is part of my job."

His job? Was that all he considered her? A responsibility? A part of his job? She drew in a breath, fighting back the disappointment, and glanced over her shoulder...and nearly wept when she saw Riley headed her way. Not having seen him since her foiled wedding day, she turned to him, held out her arms. With a bearlike growl, he scooped her up in a big hug and swung her around. "Isabelle, I swear you've put on a good ten pounds," he teased.

She fisted her hands against his shoulders. "I have not!" she cried in mortification.

He lifted a shoulder as he set her back on her feet. "Could've fooled me." He pressed a hand low on his back and winced painfully. "In fact, I think I strained something when I picked you up."

She socked a fist against his chest. "You big fake."

He grinned and caught her hand. "Come with me. There are some people who are anxious to see you."

Isabelle glanced questioningly over at Link, who stood with his arms folded across his chest, watching them. He shifted his gaze from hers to Riley, his eyes narrowing.

Riley returned the assessing gaze with one of his own. "She's my sister," he muttered resentfully. "I know how to take care of her."

Link held Riley's gaze a moment longer, the air between the two men all but sizzling, then took a step back. "See that you do."

Releasing a pent-up breath, Isabelle turned and looped her arm through her brother's. "And I have not gained weight," she informed him primly, tugging him away from Link before one of the men threw a punch.

"If you'll excuse me," Isabelle said, "I need to powder my nose."

"I'll go with you," Riley's new wife, Angelica, offered.

"Make it quick, okay?" Riley warned uneasily. "I'll wait right here."

Isabelle shot him a wicked smile, hoping to assuage his concern for her safety. "Afraid I might share some of your deep, dark secrets with Angelica?"

"He has secrets?" Angelica asked, arching a questioning brow at Riley, then tucked her arm through Isabelle's. "Do tell," she said, and led Isabelle away.

"He's wonderful," Isabelle said, laughing as she glanced back and saw the worried look on her brother's face. "But don't tell him I said so," she said confidentially. "He's hard enough to live with as it is."

"Riley?" Angelica said in surprise.

Isabelle reared back to look at her. "Don't tell me that he has you fooled?"

Angelica laughed. "No. I'm aware of his faults. And I love him, anyway."

Isabelle's heart softened at the devotion she heard in Angelica's voice.

"Angelica!"

Angelica stopped and turned, frowning. Then her face lit up. "MaryLynn!" She turned to Isabelle. "Wait right here," she said, obviously anxious to visit with her friend. "I'll just be a minute."

Isabelle shook her head, biting back a smile as she watched Angelica hurry away, then sighed, amazed at how well Angelica seemed to be holding up since her brother's death.

Sighing again, she folded her arms beneath her breasts and glanced around the room, rising to her toes as she searched for a glimpse of Link. When she didn't spot him in the crowd, she dropped back flat on her feet, disappointed, then tensed as a man's voice drifted to her. Ice spilled through her veins as the sound of it filled her mind, drawing an image of the last time she'd heard the voice. She turned slowly, searching for the source. Three men stood not thirty feet away, their heads tipped closely together, deep in conversation. She couldn't see their faces, only the profile of one.

She strained to listen as bits of the conversation floated to her.

*It's him*, she thought, her heart pounding against her ribs as the man's voice drifted to her again. One of the men she'd heard at the church. She glanced wildly around, looking for Link, then back at the group of men, just as the one facing her lifted his head and met her gaze. Her heart shot to her throat as her eyes met Brad's.

Frozen, unable to move, she stared at him, knowing that the horror of seeing him must be reflected in her eyes, in her face.

*Murderer,* was all she could think. *Murderer!*

She saw his eyes narrow, his face harden...and knew that he realized that she was aware of his guilt. He'd kill her to keep her quiet. She could see it in his eyes. In the coldness there. Link had warned her that Brad would kill her, in order to keep her quiet.

Link!

She turned, searching for him again in the crushing crowd.

When she didn't see him, she glanced back at Brad. She took a step to her right, hoping to make her way around him. But he mimicked her steps, blocking her path. She took a step to the left, and he took a step to the left, blocking that avenue of escape, as well. Feeling the panic closing in around her, she turned and did what had always gotten her into trouble in the past.

She ran away.

Her breath burned in her lungs as she ran down the empty hallway. Footsteps pounded behind her, growing closer. Ahead of her was a doorway with an exit sign lit in red. If she could make it to the doorway and outside, she told herself, she was sure she would find there one of the men from the department Link had told her was on guard.

She hit the door's bar with both hands, shoved it open and stepped out into the blinding sunlight. She blinked rapidly, looking around...but saw no one.

With her heart pounding, she spun to her left toward the front of the building...but was jerked back by an angry fist that knotted in her hair.

She screamed, the sound ripped from her throat, as pain shot through her scalp. Something sharp, unbending, pressed low on her back.

"Don't make a sound," Brad warned, his mouth close to her ear. "Just walk."

"No," she sobbed, then stumbled forward with a cry when the sharp point pierced her dress and pricked at her back. She felt the warmth of her own blood dampen her skin.

"Stupid bitch," he muttered as he shoved her ahead of him toward the parking lot. "I could've had it all."

The confidence, the evilness in his voice filled her with rage. "You killed Mike," she said angrily. "I know you did. You won't get away with his murder."

He jerked open the door to his SUV and shoved her roughly inside, sending her sprawling across the passenger seat. "They can't prove anything," he said smugly, and waved the knife at her. "Get over. You're driving."

Propped up on her elbows, Isabelle stared at the knife, frozen by fear. She had to stall, she told herself. Give Link time to discover she was missing. "Where are we going?"

He leaned inside the truck and placed the knife between her breasts. "To visit my wedding gift to you," he replied, his smile evil. "Lightfoot's Plateau Now, get behind the wheel," he ordered, increasing the knife's pressure against her skin.

"She's gone," Angelica said, her eyes wide with fear.

From the corner of his eye, Link saw two men heading for the front door. As they exited the building, the nervous dart of their gazes told Link that Isabelle had succeeded in identifying the voices.

"Find Hank," Link shouted over his shoulder to Angelica as he jogged away toward the hall where the rest rooms were located. "Tell him that Rowan's got Isabelle."

He ran, rudely shouldering his way past guests huddled together, sipping champagne and leisurely talking, and raced through the hallway and toward the double doors. When he hit the outside, he stopped, breathing hard, a knot of fear twisting in his gut when he didn't see a sign of Isabelle. Brad couldn't get far, he told himself. Link had men stationed at all the entrances to the complex.

He heard a squeal of tires, glanced toward the parking lot and saw Brad Rowan's black Navigator headed for the rear of the lot and the security fence that lined it. He glanced beyond the fence toward the red-rock plateau in the distance. "The cave," he moaned under his breath as the Navigator busted through the metal mesh and bounced over the rough terrain, dragging a panel of fencing behind it.

Link took off at a run for his Blazer.

* * *

Isabelle stumbled blindly through the dark cave, urged forward by the knife that Brad held pressed against her side. Fear held her in its grip, but she refused to give Brad the pleasure of revealing it to him.

"You won't get away with this," she said, stalling for time.

His laugh was high, bordering on demonic. "I've already gotten away with murder once. What makes you think I won't get away with it again?"

He jerked her to a stop and she spun to face him. They were in a small chamber now. Sunlight streamed through a tiny gap in the rocks above them that formed the chamber's domed ceiling, revealing his face. "Because I know what you did," she said, her voice beginning to tremble. "And so does Link."

"Templeton?" He took a threatening step toward her and placed the knife beneath her chin. "Is that where you've been?" He urged her chin up with the tip of the blade until her eyes met his. "Hiding out with Templeton?"

She saw the wildness in his eyes, the madness, and didn't doubt for a minute that he thought he could get away with murder a second time.

"He'll kill you," she whispered. "Link will find you and he will kill you, if you harm me."

His eyes darkened, hardened, and the blade pricked at her skin, making her whimper. "You're his lover, aren't you?"

When she refused to answer, he growled low in his throat. "You clung to your virginity as if it was some grand prize that I'd receive on our wedding night."

He shoved his face close to hers, the blade catching the feral gleam in his eyes. "But you didn't make Templeton wait, did you? You gave yourself to him like the whore that you are."

She felt the sting of the razor-sharp tip as it broke her skin, the warmth of the blood it drew. The coppery scent filled her nose, shot fear through her veins. With her eyes riveted on Brad's, she took a step back. Rocks crumbled beneath her feet and she bit back a scream, grabbing for him to keep from falling.

"Careful," he said, closing his fingers brutally around her arm. "You might fall and hurt yourself." He leaned around her to peer at the dark pit behind her. He kicked a rock over the edge, listened until he heard it strike the rocks below, then laughed when the whir of hundreds of rattlers answered.

Rattlesnakes! A shudder quaked through her and she squeezed her eyes shut, remembering the stories her brothers had told her about the rattlers that nested in the pit. She swallowed hard, pushing back the fear the memory drew, then opened her eyes again to meet Brad's gaze. "Killing me will not save you," she told him fiercely. "Link knows you murdered Mike. You may kill me, but you won't save yourself in doing so."

"And who'll believe him? Hmm?" he quizzed, stroking the point of the knife down the smooth column of her neck. "I saw the file your daddy's been building on Templeton. The guilt of Templeton's relatives will throw enough suspicion on whatever claims he makes about me to make people doubt his word. Besides," he said, and stroked the point of the knife back up, forcing her chin higher. ''Your death will be almost expected. Poor thing,'' he murmured, puckering his lips sympathetically. ''You're already the talk of the town. Everyone knows you are emotionally unstable. You skipping out on our wedding only proved to them how unstable you really are. I'll simply explain that, upon seeing me at the dedication, you realized what a mistake you'd made, lured me to this cave to beg my forgiveness and reestablish our relationship. When I refused to reconcile with you, you became hysterical and, though I tried desperately to stop you, you leaped to your death among the rattlesnakes.''

''They'll know I was murdered,'' she said, her eyes wide and unblinking as they met the madness in his. ''They'll see the evidence, and it will point to you.''

''What evidence?'' he asked innocently. He turned the blade of the knife and grinned when she flinched at the pain. ''I'm not going to lay a hand on you. You're going to jump and those rattlers are going to do the job for me. Ever been snakebit, Isabelle?'' he asked, then laughed when she whimpered pitifully, shrinking as far away from him as the knife would allow. ''They'll be all over you within seconds. You'll die a slow, miserable death all alone.''

''No, she won't.''

Brad whirled at the sound of Link's voice but managed to keep the knife pressed against Isabelle's throat. ''Well, well, well,'' he said, smiling as he eyed the barrel of the .38 Link had leveled on his chest. ''If it isn't Pueblo's most dedicated public servant, Link Templeton.'' He eased closer to Isabelle's side and curved an arm around her waist, using her body as a shield. With the knife, he tipped her chin higher, while holding her against his side. "Why don't you put down that gun, Templeton?" he suggested easily. "It makes me kind of nervous. My hands shake when I'm nervous," he added, then smiled. "It'd be a shame if I accidentally sliced Isabelle's throat."

"No, Link!" Isabelle cried. "Don't listen to him. Shoot him! Please! Just shoot him!"

Link tore his gaze from Brad's to meet Isabelle's. He saw the fear in the violet depths, the desperation. Another time, he might have weighed his chances, called Brad's bluff. But not this time. Not when Isabelle's life was at stake. Slowly he lowered the gun, then tossed it to the ground.

"That's better," Brad said with a pleased smile.

"For who?" Link growled. "Certainly not for you. I heard all you told Isabelle. Now you have *two* witnesses to kill. You'll never get away with it, Rowan. You might have been able to escape the blame for one death, but never two."

"Oh, but I will," Brad replied confidently, his smile widening. "In fact, this makes the scenario even more believable. I'll just change my story a bit. Explain to everyone that Isabelle got cold feet prior to our wedding. Understandable," he said, with a sympathetic look Isabelle's way, "considering the poor dear's fragile emotional state. A kidnapping does leave its mark on a child," he added, arching a pointed brow at Link.

When Link remained silent, refusing to rise to the bait, Brad sighed and continued. "As the time drew near for our wedding ceremony to begin, Isabelle grew more and more distraught, more unstable. She was a virgin, after all, and fearful of her wedding night. So, she ran away...and straight into the arms of one of Pueblo's finest.'' He lifted a shoulder. ''Of course, once everyone learns of your history and your involvement in the first kidnapping, it won't be difficult to convince them that you've held a grudge all these years and were determined to make Isabelle pay for the time your stepbrother has spent behind bars.''

''No!'' Isabelle cried. ''Don't listen to him, Link! No one will ever believe him.''

Brad lifted a brow. ''Won't they?'' He smiled at Link. ''What do you think? Think the D.A. can come up with the evidence he needs to convict me? Think he can prove, without a shadow of doubt, that I killed both you and Isabelle? Don't you think there might be just one juror who might be affected by your past? By your association with known felons and kidnappers? Don't you think there's just the slightest chance that I might get away with murder a second time?''

When Link remained silent, Brad laughed, the demonic sound echoing around them in the cave's chamber. He kept the knife tipped beneath Isabelle's chin, the sharp blade curved toward her neck, and gave his own chin a slight jerk, indicating the pit behind him. ''Do you know what's down there, Templeton? Rattlesnakes,'' he said smugly, not waiting for an answer. ''Hundreds of them just waiting to greet you, to sink their fangs into your flesh. I'll be a hero for trying to save Isabelle from you.''

Link never once took his eyes off Brad's face. To

do so, to spare even one look at Isabelle, would break his concentration, jeopardize whatever chance he might have to save her. "Then what?" Link posed. "If I fall into the pit and the snakes kill me, how will you explain Isabelle's death? No one will believe that we both fell into the pit, while you walk out alive, unharmed."

Brad arched a brow. "Did I fail to mention that Isabelle will die of a gunshot? To her heart," he clarified, then nodded toward the pistol lying on the floor of the cave. "And from your gun. You went crazy when you saw Isabelle leave the dedication with me and followed us here. You shot her in a jealous rage. I fought with you, trying to wrestle the gun away from you before you could kill me, too. Unfortunately, you lost your balance in the struggle and fell into the pit. The perfect crime," he said, his smile broadening. "Wouldn't you agree?"

When Link didn't respond, Brad lifted his hand slightly from Isabelle's waist, gesturing for Link to join them at the edge of the pit. "Now, come along. Time's a-wasting. And my hand is growing stiff from holding this knife to Isabelle's throat. Keep your distance, though," he warned. "If you should get too close, I might become nervous and my hand might slip. We wouldn't want that to happen, now, would we?" His gaze on Link, measuring his response, he pressed the razor-sharp point of the knife against Isabelle's skin. A drop of blood swelled around the tip and dropped onto his hand. He laughed, the sound that of a maniac, a cold-blooded killer.

Link kept his gaze leveled on Brad, steeling him-

self against the sound of Isabelle's sob as the blade
nicked her flesh, sending a fresh stream of blood
coursing down her neck. He locked his emotions
away, kept his expression blank and focused his mind
on escape, searching for a way to get Isabelle out of
the cave alive. He had but two weapons available to
him. His fists and his gun. But his gun lay on the
ground out of reach. The five or so feet between it
and his feet stretched like a mile.

He mentally pictured himself making a dive for it,
lifting the gun and aiming it at Brad's chest, pulling
the trigger. He'd have only seconds to accomplish the
move. In his mind's eye, he could see Brad's face,
slack with surprise, his eyes wide as the bullet burned
a path through his chest. Brad pitching backward over
the edge of the pit, driven by the force of the bullet.
The thud of his body striking the rocks far below.

But if he succeeded in getting his hands on the gun,
would he be endangering Isabelle more? Link asked
himself. If he managed to get off a shot, would Brad
take Isabelle with him into the pit when he fell?

Link couldn't be sure. And it was that uncertainty
that made him hesitate, his gaze locked on Brad's.
Help was coming, he told himself. Riley would find
Hank and tell him that Rowan had Isabelle and that
Link had gone after them. Hank would see the hole
in the fence that Brad's vehicle had left, and he would
know where Brad had taken Isabelle, just as Link had
known. It was just a matter of time before Hank arrived at Lightfoot's Plateau.

Link just had to stall a while longer.

# Eight

Link took a step toward the pit, pretending to follow Brad's instructions. "Why'd you kill Mike, Brad?"

Brad's upper lip curled in a snarl. "What difference does it make? Dead is dead. Dodd's no longer an issue."

Link lifted a shoulder but kept walking, keeping his steps slow and cautious, fighting for time. "Just curious. Seems stupid to have killed him. If money was your only goal, you had the perfect setup. You were stealing the Fortunes blind right beneath their noses. Embezzling funds from the hospital construction site. Pretty clever scheme."

Brad's expression turned smug. "Which became unnecessary to continue once Isabelle agreed to marry me. My marriage to her would have assured me a free hand in the Fortune coffers."

Isabelle's shriek of fury took both Brad and Link by surprise. Before either could recover, she whacked her hand across Brad's arm, knocking the knife away from her throat and out of his hand. It clattered against the rocks at his feet.

Cursing, Brad grabbed for her as she lunged for the gun, managed to grab a fistful of her dress and yanked her back as he stooped to snatch the dropped knife from the ground.

Seeing an opportunity, perhaps the only one he'd have to save Isabelle, Link made a wild dive for Brad. His chest slammed against Rowan's shoulder, breaking the man's hold on Isabelle.

"Run!" Link yelled as he closed a hand around Brad's wrist and slammed it down hard against the rocks. As she scrambled away, he squeezed his fingers around Brad's wrist, grinding his teeth as he strained to break Brad's grip on the knife.

Brad struggled beneath him and managed to ram an elbow into Link's chest. Link choked, gasping, as his breath whooshed out of him. Using the advantage, Brad humped his back and sent Link stumbling back a step, then leaped to his feet with a growl and whirled to face Link, his arms held out at his sides, the knife clutched tightly in his right hand. They circled, their eyes locked on each other. Brad lunged, stabbing wildly at Link, but Link dodged the blade and locked a hand around Brad's wrist again, shoving it high in the air. Chest to chest, they strained for control of the knife.

"Drop the knife, Brad, or I'll shoot."

At the sound of Isabelle's voice, Link glanced over

to see her standing a few feet away, both hands gripped tightly around his pistol's butt, its barrel aimed at Brad's chest.

Brad snorted at her threat. "You haven't got the guts," he sneered.

She narrowed her eyes, her finger trembling on the trigger. "That's what you think."

Just as she squeezed the trigger, Brad leaped back, jerking Link with him. The sound of the gun's explosive blast blended with Isabelle's scream as Link caught the bullet she'd meant for Brad.

Pain burned through Link, stunning him for a moment, his ears ringing with the pistol's loud report. He could hear Isabelle's scream echoing around him, her broken sobs, the sound of metal striking stone as she dropped the gun to the ground, all of it sounding as if it came from a long distance away. He couldn't quit, he told himself, feeling the seductive darkness sucking at him. Not until Isabelle was safe. Sweat broke out on his forehead and he set his jaw, tightened his grip on Brad's wrist, twisted higher.

Rock shifted beneath his feet and he blinked furiously, trying to keep Brad's swimming face in focus as they fought for control of the knife. The pit, he remembered dully as he felt his left foot slide toward its edge. They were standing at the edge of the pit. One wrong move and they would both go over the rim.

He shook his head, trying to clear the webs that clouded his vision, his mind, knowing that he had to stay alert, that he couldn't give in to the pain. If he did, Brad would win.

And Isabelle would die.

A hand closed around his throat, fingers squeezing brutally around his windpipe, cutting off his air. He tried to raise his free hand to fend off the attack, but his arm wouldn't cooperate, hung limply at his side. Darkness pushed at him from every direction and he could feel his knees weakening, the strength leaking from his body right along with the blood that leaked from the wound in his chest. His grip on Brad's wrist weakened, slipped, and Brad jerked free, releasing his hold on Link's neck as he took a step back. Gasping, Link dropped weakly to his hands and knees, his head bowed low as he tried to draw in much-needed air.

"You're going to die, Templeton," Brad warned darkly as he lifted the knife high, preparing to embed the blade in Link's back.

"No!" Isabelle screamed, and ran forward, dropping to the ground beside Link and throwing her arms around him to protect him from the blow.

"Drop the knife, Rowan."

Brad whirled at the barked command to find Hank standing where Isabelle had stood only moments before. But the quick move was his downfall. His eyes shot wide, his arms arcing out, as the ground beneath his feet began to crumble. He flapped his arms wildly, trying to regain a footing. His terror-filled scream rent the air as he pitched backward and the darkness swallowed him whole.

His breath coming in hard, pain-filled gasps, Link tugged Isabelle's head against his neck, covering her ear with his palm to block out the nightmarish sound of Brad's scream.

Seconds later, the thud of Brad's body against the rocks below silenced his scream, though the sound continued to echo around the cave's chamber, blending eerily with that of the deadly snakes' rattles as they moved in for the kill.

Then there was only silence.

"You okay?"

Link glanced up to find Hank stooped over him, his face creased with concern. Four uniformed policemen stood behind him. Link opened his mouth to answer, but closed it again as nausea rose. He dropped his hand from Isabelle. "Get her out of here." He barely managed to choke the words out. "She needs a doctor."

Hank hunkered down and caught Isabelle by the shoulders and tried to ease her away from Link.

"No," she cried, clinging to him. "I'm staying with Link."

"Take it easy," Hank soothed as he pried her fingers from around Link's neck. "I just need to see how badly you're hurt." He took one look at the blood smeared on Isabelle's neck and that which soaked her dress and glanced over his shoulder at the four men behind him, giving his head a jerk. Two of the men immediately turned and headed for the entrance to the cave.

Hank stood, wrapped an arm around Isabelle's waist and drew her to her feet. "I want you to go with these men, Isabelle," he ordered firmly.

She tugged free and dropped to her knees again, wrapping her arms around Link and burying her face in the curve of his neck. "No," she sobbed. "He's hurt. It's my fault. I shot him."

Squeezing his eyes shut at the guilt he heard in her voice, Link dipped his head lower between his elbows as she clung to him. The pain currently knifing through him had nothing to do with the bullet Isabelle had unintentionally fired into him and everything to do with the woman who held him, her tears scalding his neck. He wanted so badly to haul her into his arms, cover her face with kisses, bury his face in her hair and inhale her sweetness. He'd almost lost her. If he'd arrived even seconds later, Brad might have already killed her, sent her plunging to her death into the pit of rattlesnakes. A shudder racked his body at the thought.

But she wasn't his to lose, he reminded himself. She was a Fortune. And he was a nobody. He hauled in a ragged breath and forced his eyes open.

His job had been to protect her from Brad Rowan, he told himself.

And now his job was done.

Drawing deep for the strength he'd need to do what he knew needed to be done, he sank back on his heels, grimacing at the pain that seared through him as he reached to drag her arms from around his neck. "Go home, Isabelle," he growled, and pushed her away. "Go back to your royal castle where you belong."

Her face paled even more as she stared at him. "No, Link, please—"

"Go!" he shouted, waving her away. "I don't want you here."

He turned his face away, unable to bear the ravaged

look in her eyes, the tears that streamed down her face. He squeezed his own eyes shut as he listened to the faint rustle of her dress on the stone as she struggled to her feet, her strangled sob as she turned and hurried away.

On a moan, he fell forward, planting his hands against the ground, curling his fingers against the rough stone.

Hank sank down to a knee beside his bent form and placed a hand gently on his shoulder. "How bad is it, buddy?"

Link squeezed his eyes shut. "The gunshot wound?" he asked, then gulped a breath. "Or my heart?"

Link stood in front of the sliding door in his condominium, staring out at his postage-stamp-size backyard. The arrests of the two men who had been in on the scam with Rowan, working from inside Fortune Construction and falsifying purchase orders for materials used in the construction of the children's hospital, thus embezzling funds from Fortune Construction, were now behind bars. Though not directly involved in the murder of Mike Dodd, their knowledge and silence made them accessories to the crime and had posed a potential threat to Isabelle until they were apprehended. Sighing, Link braced an arm high on the door frame. The other was strapped against his chest in a sling. Beneath it, tape bound his chest. He'd been lucky, the doctors had told him. The bullet had entered his left arm just below his shoulder, exited after tearing through some muscle and nerves, then reentered his body, shattering a rib.

A little nerve damage. A busted rib. Not much damage when compared to what the bullet could have done. Nothing if compared to the pain in his heart.

He straightened, trying to shake off the thoughts of Isabelle before they could fully form. But they stubbornly pushed themselves into his mind, shaping themselves into images that grew stronger with each ragged breath he drew. Waking to find her sitting beside his hospital bed, her fingers gripped tightly around his. The gauze and tape on her neck that covered the wounds Brad had inflicted with his knife. The paleness of her face. The guilt that haunted her violet eyes.

He'd stared at her for a moment, memorizing each detail of her face, regret a lead weight on his chest, before he'd pulled his hand from hers and turned his face away.

He'd heard her whispered, tear-filled "I'm sorry" and wanted desperately to tell her that he didn't blame her for the bullet he'd taken. That he loved her more than life itself. Instead, he'd clamped his lips together and stared at the view beyond the window until he'd heard the door close softly behind her. His view of the hospital parking lot had blurred a bit when he heard her leave, knowing that he'd probably never see her again. Never touch her. Never hold her. Never...

The doorbell rang, interrupting his thoughts, but he ignored it, hoping whoever it was would go away. It rang again and he swore, angling his head to glare at the front door. It rang a third time and he spun to march across the room. He jerked open the door, snarling.

Kate Fortune, the matriarch of the Fortune family, stood on the small stoop, her finger poised over the bell to ring it again. She straightened and arched a regal brow as she raked her gaze over Link, noting his scraggly appearance. "Well!" she said with a sniff of disapproval. "I certainly would have thought that you'd have recuperated enough after three weeks to properly dress yourself and shave."

Link dragged a hand self-consciously over his jaw, two days of stubble scraping against his palm. He dropped his hand and scowled. "What do you want?"

She pushed a hand against his chest as she swept past him and into his living room. "To talk to you."

His scowl deepened as he watched her stop and glance curiously around. "About what?" he growled rudely, and slammed the door.

She turned to peer at him. "About my Isabelle."

"What about her?"

She arched a brow. "Aren't you going to invite me to sit down?"

Link scowled at the reminder of his lack of manners but gestured toward the sofa. "Sit."

She pursed her lips. "Why, thank you. I believe I will."

Anxious to send the woman on her way, Link pushed himself away from the wall. "You said you wanted to talk about Isabelle."

"Yes," she agreed with a brisk nod. "Though she wouldn't be very happy if she knew I was here. She's a bit like you," she said, and gave him a pointed look over her brow. "Stubborn as a mule and just as thick-headed."

Link snorted. "Isabelle?" At her nod, he shook his head. "You don't know her very well. She's as meek as a lamb."

"Really?" Kate drawled, then laughed. "I guess it's true, then. Love really is blind."

Link tensed. "Who said anything about love?"

"Well, I did, you silly man," she scolded. "And if you had any sense at all, you'd realize that Isabelle is head over heels in love with you, as well."

Link slapped a hand against the back of his neck and paced away. "She just thinks she is. She'll get over it."

"Oh, I doubt that. A Fortune doesn't fall in love easily, *or* foolishly," she added sagely.

Link whirled to glare at her. "Well, she was a fool if she fell in love with me." He tossed out a hand, gesturing wildly at the sparsely decorated room. "Look around you, Mrs. Fortune. Is this the kind of life you would want for Isabelle?" He sliced his hand through the air, cutting off her response before she could offer it. "Marrying me wouldn't be a step down the social ladder. It would be a nosedive all the way to the bottom. Hell," he said, tossing his hand high. "She'd be crying to Daddy to let her come back home before the ink was even dry on the marriage certificate."

Kate rose, her face flushed with anger, her lips pinched tightly together. "How dare you insult Isabelle in such a way! If she has a shortcoming, it is her innocence. And *that* is the fault of her family," she added, "not her own."

"Yes, she's innocent. But *I'm* not," he added, stabbing a thumb against his chest. "I *know* what it's like to go hungry. To lie in bed shivering with cold because the electricity has been turned off. To have people look at me with pity because my shoes were worn out and my pants full of holes. And I'd *never* subject Isabelle to that kind of life. Never," he repeated emphatically.

"Would you love Isabelle if she were poor?"

He stared at her in stupefaction, then slapped a hand against the back of his neck and spun away. "Doesn't matter. She's rich as sin."

"Oh, I think it does matter," she insisted. "If it didn't, you would answer my question. Would you love her if she were poor?"

"Of course I would love her!" he shouted, turning to glare at her. "I will always love her."

"Yet, you think that Isabelle's feelings for you would dissipate if you suddenly lost your ability to support her, that she would go running home to her daddy." She arched a brow. "And you suggested that Isabelle was prejudiced?" She made a tsking sound with her tongue. "*You're* the one with prejudices," she scolded, "refusing to give her your heart just because she happens to come from a wealthy family."

She stood. "Don't let stubbornness stand between you and happiness," she warned sternly, then sighed and shook her head sadly. "It can," she told him. "I know, because I allowed it to stand between my husband and me for too many years." Her lips curved in a soft smile as she crossed to him. "Isabelle loves with her heart." She tapped a manicured nail against his chest. "It's what's inside a man that's important to her. Not the size of his bank account."

That same afternoon, Isabelle stood at the window, her gaze fixed on her mother's rose garden, trying her best to shut out the conversation going on behind her.

"Well, something has to be done," she heard her father shout. "Templeton saved Isabelle's life and that act alone demands some sort of response from this family."

"I'm as indebted to the man as you," Riley replied tersely. "I merely suggested that offering him the job of head of security for Fortune Construction might not be the best way to show our gratitude."

Weary of hearing Link's name bandied about by her family, sure that she'd scream at even one more reminder of the man who had broken her heart, Isabelle turned away from the window to face her family. "He won't accept the job, even if you offer it to him."

Her father looked at her in surprise. "And why not?" he demanded, insulted.

"Because he considers what he did a part of his job. Nothing more." She shifted her gaze to her brother Riley and tried to keep the bitterness from her voice when she added, "So there's no need for you to worry about employing a man you obviously despise."

"I don't despise him," Riley said defensively. "It was you I was thinking of. I'm sure that it would be difficult for you to be around the man, considering what all transpired between the two of you."

Isabelle curled her hands into fists at her sides and drew in a breath. "What *transpired* between Link and me is none of your business," she told her brother furiously. "And I'm weary of this family trying to shield me from any unpleasantries," she added, whirling to glare at each member of her family in turn. "I'm a grown woman and fully capable of taking care of myself."

"Isabelle's right."

Every head in the room turned to peer at Kate Fortune, who, up until that point, had remained unusually quiet throughout the discussion. As the matriarch of the family, her opinions were respected, as well as valued, but the fact that she had sided with Isabelle on this issue took them all by surprise.

Kate gave her chin an imperious lift. "You've pro tected her long enough. She's no longer your responsibility. She's grown and fully capable of caring for herself."

Stunned by Kate's pronouncement, Isabelle took a moment to recover. When she did, she crossed to the woman and dropped to a knee in front of her, taking her hand in hers. "Thank you, Kate."

Kate smiled fondly and patted Isabelle's hand. "No thanks needed, dear. You've earned your independence. And your actions in the cave proved that you're more than capable of handling anything that comes your way."

"I still believe we owe Templeton some expression of our gratitude," Hunter Fortune grumbled.

Kate turned her gaze to her stepson. "Then why not give him his due?" she asked him. "Something he can accept, without offending his pride, or his conscience?"

A week after Kate Fortune's visit to his house, Link returned to work, relieved to have something to focus on besides his loss of Isabelle.

"Templeton!"

Link lifted his head from the lab report on his desk to find Chief Luben standing in his office doorway. "Yeah, boss?"

"The mayor wants you in his office at ten."

"But this is my first day back on the job," Link argued.

"I've got appointments scheduled all morning."

Luben turned back to his office. "Cancel 'em," he ordered, and slammed his door behind him.

Link glanced over at Hank. "What the hell was that all about?"

Hank lifted a shoulder. "Beats me." He grinned and reached behind him, tugging a tie from the hat rack. "The city's probably gonna give you some kind of award for bravery or something. More than likely, reporters will be there from the paper, taking pictures. Maybe a news crew from the TV station." He tossed Link the tie, his grin widening. "I'm sure you'll want to look your best."

Link scowled and wadded up the tie and threw it back at Hank. "Like I give a damn how I look," he muttered disagreeably as he walked out the door and headed for the mayor's office.

* * *

Still wearing a scowl, Link stepped into the mayor's office at precisely ten o'clock.

The mayor's secretary looked up from her computer monitor and smiled when she saw him. "Hi, Link. How are you feeling?"

He lifted the arm still bound inside the sling, his scowl deepening. "I'll feel better when they cut me loose from this thing."

She laughed as she rose. "I'll bet it's difficult to dress when you've only got the use of one hand."

"I get by," he muttered, then jerked his head toward the mayor's closed office door. "Is he in?"

"Yes," she replied, and led the way to the door. She pushed it open, then smiled up at Link as she held it for him. "Everyone else has already arrived."

"Everyone?" he repeated, tensing.

She laughed softly and gave him a nudge inside. "Yes, everyone," she whispered, and closed the door behind him.

Link glanced uneasily around the crowded room, his stomach tightening when Hunter Fortune stepped from the group of men gathered near the door, blocking his view of the rest of the room's occupants.

"Hello, Link," Hunter said, smiling warmly as he extended a hand in welcome. "It's good to see you again."

Link clasped the man's hand in his and shook. "Mr. Fortune," he mumbled by way of greeting.

"How's that arm?" Hunter asked, nodding toward Link's sling.

Link lifted a shoulder as he peered around Hunter

and met Riley's intense gaze. "It's okay," he said as he slid his gaze to meet that of Shane. Unlike their father, neither of Fortune's sons appeared very happy to see Link. "Is this meeting going to take long?" Link asked, anxious to get whatever business needed tending out of the way so that he could leave. Being trapped inside a room full of Fortunes was making him more than a little uncomfortable.

Hunter stepped aside and swung his arm wide, gesturing for Link to precede him. "Not long at all," he assured him. "Just have a seat here next to Isabelle."

Link stopped short when Isabelle turned in her chair to look up at him. He'd told himself that he'd forget her. That whatever feelings he'd thought he'd had for her would dim over time. But the sudden kick of his pulse as their gazes met, the sudden dryness in his mouth, the heat that raced through his veins, let him know that four weeks hadn't been long enough. As he stared into her violet eyes, he wasn't sure that a lifetime would be long enough to forget her.

He heard the mayor clear his throat and tore his gaze from hers, then dropped down into the chair next to hers. He slouched down and stretched out his legs, crossing them at the ankles. "What's up, Mayor?" he asked with a nonchalance that defied the thundering of his pulse, the tremble in the hand he fisted on the chair's arm.

The mayor beamed a smile. "Hunter has a little presentation he'd like to make."

Link was on his feet before the mayor could say anything more. He planted his hand on the mayor's desk and leaned across it to glare at the man. "If this is some kind of award or something," he said angrily, "I don't want it. What I did in that cave, I did because it was my job. And the bullet I took is a risk I take every day on the street while I'm doing that job."

A hand closed over his shoulder and he whirled, shrugging off the hand to glare at Riley, who'd made the mistake of placing it there. Riley lifted his hands in surrender and backed away, saying, "If you'll give us time to explain."

Link rolled his shoulders defensively. "All right," he said reluctantly, and sat back down. "But make it fast. I've got work to do."

Hunter stepped forward. "We have some old business to tend to." He slipped a hand inside his suit jacket and pulled out an envelope. He stared at it, frowning as he tapped it against his hand. "Eighteen years ago," he began slowly, "I offered a reward for information that would lead to the safe return of my daughter. Though I received the information I needed, the man who offered it never stepped forward to claim the reward." He flipped open the envelope and pulled out a check. "A million dollars," he said, and glanced down at Link. "That was the reward I offered. You earned it, son," he said, and pushed the check onto the palm of Link's injured hand, forcing him to take it.

Link stared at the check, the long line of zeroes following the number one. A million dollars. More money than he'd seen in his whole life. Probably more than he'd hold in his hands at any one time, no matter how hard he worked, or how long he lived.

And Hunter Fortune was giving it to him for making a damn phone call.

He shook his head slowly at the irony in that, then jerked his head up to peer at Hunter as the man pressed another check into his hand.

"And this check," Hunter explained, "represents the bonus offered by Fortune Construction Company for the capture of Mike Dodd's murderer."

Link stared down at the check, the zeroes dancing before his eyes. A million dollars. His gut constricted in denial. He'd done nothing to earn the money. He'd merely done his job. And he hadn't captured Brad Rowan. Rowan had died in that cave, a result of his own greed and stupidity, not by any effort on Link's part to subdue him.

Two million dollars, he thought as he continued to stare at the slips of paper resting on his upturned palm. The money would go a long way in shortening the gap that stretched between him and Isabelle. With it, he could offer her a semblance of the life she'd always known.

He glanced up and met the gaze of Kate Fortune, who stood slightly behind the mayor and to his left. Kate shifted her gaze discreetly to Isabelle, then back to Link's, arching a brow as if asking him what he was going to do about Isabelle now that he was a multimillionaire. He stared at Kate a moment longer...and a smile began to grow inside him, working its way to his lips.

He turned to look at Isabelle, who was staring straight ahead, her back rigid, her face void of any emotion. The smile slowly melted from his face. He'd hurt her, he reminded himself when she stubbornly refused to meet his gaze. She'd offered him her love and he'd tossed it back in her face, just as she'd accused him of doing.

"You said you loved me."

She whipped her head around to meet his gaze, her eyes narrowed dangerously.

"Did you mean it?" he asked quietly.

"Now, listen here," Riley began to say angrily from behind him.

Link held up a hand, silencing her brother, but kept his gaze locked on Isabelle's. "Did you?" he asked again. "Did you mean it when you said you loved me?"

A frown pleated her forehead and she swallowed, then slowly nodded her head. "Yes. I meant it."

"Do you still?"

Tears filled her eyes and she nodded again. "Yes."

He twisted around in his chair to fully face her. "And would you still love me if I was broke?"

"Yes," she said tearfully. "I'd love you even then."

He rose to stand facing her. With his gaze on hers, he took the checks her father had given him and tore them in two, rearranged the pieces, then tore them again. He tossed the shredded paper into the air, then dropped to a knee in front of her as the pieces rained down around him like confetti.

"I love you, Isabelle Fortune," he said, taking her hand in his. "And I promise to love you through thick and thin, to protect you and keep you safe until the day I die." He tightened his fingers around hers, looking deeply into her eyes. "I want you to marry me. Be my wife. I don't have much, but what I have is mine. I worked hard for it, and I want to share it with you."

Link watched her lips tremble, the tears spill over her lower lids, and had never known a fear like the one that held him in its grip while he waited for her answer.

"Well, say something!" Kate cried.

Isabelle glanced at Kate, took a deep breath, then slowly brought her gaze back to Link's. "And I love you," she said, her voice trembling. She dipped her chin and drew in a long breath, swallowed, then lifted her head and squared her shoulders as she met his gaze. "I promise to love you through thick and thin," she said, offering back to him the same assurances he'd offered her. "And I promise to protect you," she told him, her voice growing stronger as did her conviction, "and keep you safe until the day I die."

Link stared at her, absorbing her words, the strength behind them, the determination, and mentally compared the confident woman who sat opposite him to the meek and seemingly helpless woman he'd rescued from a car in the desert little more than a month before. As he searched her eyes, he saw the truth there, and he knew without a doubt that she meant what she said, that she loved him, would stand with him, beside him, no matter what.

"Marry me," he whispered, gripping her hand more tightly in his. "Please say you'll marry me."

"Yes." She flung herself against Link's chest and her arms around his neck, forcing him to brace a hand against the floor to keep them both from tumbling over backward, while she cried, laughing, "Yes, yes, yes!"

Link strained to support their weight with the strength of the one arm he held braced against the floor. "Hold on a second," he mumbled, and eased Isabelle back onto her chair. He slowly heaved himself to his feet and blew out a long breath, then smiled down at her.

"Let's try that again," he said as he slipped his arm from the sling and ripped the encumbrance over his head. He winced only slightly as he flexed his arm, easing the stiffness from it, then tossed the sling aside and opened his arms wide.

"Say it again," he instructed.

"What?" she said in confusion.

"Say it again," he repeated impatiently. "When you say yes this time, I want to be able to hold you with *both* my arms."

"Yes," she said, rising to her feet to face him. "Yes," she said again as she stepped within the circle of his embrace. "Yes," she murmured one last time before lifting her hands and drawing his face down to hers.

Kate chuckled as she looked on the tender scene. "Hunter, looks as if you'll be paying for another wedding before long."

Hunter smiled, his chest swelling a bit. "Yes, it seems as if I will."

# Epilogue

**R**adiant in a simple gown of ivory satin that billowed around her legs, stirred by the soft wind that blew across the plateau, Isabelle gazed up at Link as he repeated his vows to her. They stood facing each other, hands joined between them, before the entrance to the cave on Lightfoot's Plateau, just as Isabelle's great-grandmother Fiona had pledged her love to her beloved Joseph Fortune.

A century of history and love, Kate Fortune acknowledged silently, pleased by the thought as she stood to the left of Isabelle, honored that she'd asked her to serve as her matron of honor. Though others in the family had offered their concerns about Isabelle and Link repeating their vows at the cave, Kate had pooh-poohed their skepticism, which had surprised everyone…but no one more than Kate, herself. Lightfoot's Plateau stood as a bold reminder of her husband's infidelity and the twin sons that resulted from his affair with Natasha Lightfoot. But Kate was a realist, a strong and confident woman, she liked to think, who refused to allow a situation or a piece of property to threaten her happiness. And she was happy, she thought smugly, having made her peace with her husband over his disloyalty, and eventually recognizing his sons, Devlin and Hunter, before her husband's death.

She was proud of Ben's sons and their children, but never more at this moment, as she stood amongst them all, witnessing Isabelle and Link's wedding vows. To her it seemed only fitting that the two should pledge their love to each other on the spot that legend told would sanctify their union with a love so pure as to last a lifetime.

And so what if Brad Rowan had died within the bowels of the cave? Kate asked herself with a sniff of disdain. Isabelle and Link had not caused the man's death. The foolish and greedy man had brought his untimely and gruesome demise upon himself. And Kate stubbornly believed that it was Isabelle's experience in the cave that fateful afternoon that had given her the courage to shrug off her family's determination to protect her from life itself, and claim her rightful place as a strong, mature woman within the Fortune family, with a mind and heart of her own.

While the priest offered his blessings over the couple, Kate glanced around, her smile growing proud as her gaze settled on first Jason and his new bride, Adele, then moved on to Jason's brother, Tyler, and his wife, Julie. With a sigh of the purest contentment, she swept her gaze to look with approval at Ben's handsome twin grandsons—Riley, standing with his arm curved protectively around his wife Angelica's waist, then Shane, standing proudly beside his wife, Cynthia, a wide hand braced on the shoulder of his young son, Bobbie. A son Shane was a little slow in claiming as his own, she thought, arching a disapproving brow.

She sighed heavily, turning her gaze back to the couple who stood at the entrance to the cave, heads bowed reverently, fingers locked in a symbol of their union as one. It would seem, she reflected sadly as she studied the two, that the Fortunes would be forever plagued with difficulties in finding, then finally joining with the proper mate.

She smiled as she watched Isabelle lift her face and Link lower his for the traditional kiss, sealing their union, a marriage of souls linked for eternity. Pleasure filled her heart, spilled over to soothe her soul as she nodded her approval.

But things usually worked out in the end, she told herself, then sniffed back tears as she slipped a paper from the sleeve of her dress. She approached the newlyweds, still locked in a tight embrace—a kiss that had stretched on a bit too long, in her estimation. "Enough of that mushy nonsense," she grumped. "I have a wedding gift for the two of you."

Isabelle laughed as a blush worked its way up Link's neck, staining his cheeks, then wrapped an arm around his waist and hugged him to her side as she turned to look at Kate. "But you've already given us a wedding gift," she reminded gently. "Remember?"

Kate humphed and gave her chin an indignant lift. "I may be old, but I'm not senile. I know very well that I've already given you a wedding gift, and I'll give you another, if I so choose. But this gift," she added, holding up the piece of paper, "isn't from me. It's from the Rowans."

The blood drained from Isabelle's face and she took a step back. "From the Rowans?"

"Yes," Kate acknowledged, and pushed the paper against Isabelle's hand, forcing Isabelle to take it. "Though I was as hesitant as you when the Rowans first approached me with it. But after giving their gift some thought, I decided that it was appropriate, fitting, even. Open it," she insisted, waving an impatient hand toward the document Isabelle held. "See for yourself."

Her fingers shaking, Isabelle unfolded the document and quickly scanned it, her eyes widening. "But it's the deed to Lightfoot's Plateau," she cried.

Kate nodded her head in agreement. "Yes, it is. The Rowans wanted to give the land back to the Fortunes, a way of making amends for all the pain and suffering their son inflicted upon this family. And who better to hold the deed than the couple whose happiness he most threatened."

Tears filled Isabelle's eyes and she dropped her gaze to stare at the deed again. "Lightfoot's Plateau," she whispered, then lifted her gaze to meet that of her husband's. "It's ours," she said, linking her fingers with his.

"Yours," he corrected her.

"Oh, for heaven's sake," Kate groused. "When you marry, you become one. Hearts, souls *and* possessions," she added with a decisive nod of her head.

"Yes, ma'am," Link murmured dutifully, though he bit back a smile as he met the old woman's gaze.

Kate gave a sniff. "That's better. Just proves that you're not too old to learn a few manners, young man. Respect for the elderly is a virtue," she informed him primly. "One you'd be wise to practice."

"Oh, I have the utmost respect for you, Mrs. Fortune," Link assured her, then glanced down at Isabelle and shot her a wink. "In fact," he said, stepping forward, "I might even be a bit in love with you."

Kate's eyes shot wide in dismay. "You what!"

Link tossed back his head and laughed, then scooped Kate up into his arms and twirled her around. After spinning a fast circle, he set her back down on her feet, then bussed her a quick kiss on the lips. "In a familial way, of course," he assured her as he looped his arm through hers, then crooked his other in invitation to Isabelle. He escorted them toward the fleet of limousines that waited to deliver the wedding party to the Fortune estate and a reception already touted as surpassing in grandeur the previous reception her parents had planned. "I know how to keep the ladies in my life safe, don't I, sweetheart?" he asked, glancing down at Isabelle for her confirmation.

Isabelle tilted up her face for his kiss. "Oh, yes," she said, sighing. "You've done an excellent job of keeping me safe." She shifted her face close to his ear and nipped at his earlobe before adding suggestively, "But there is one thing that you do much, much better...."

Link groaned as her tongue swept over the shell of his ear and quickened his pace toward the car, making both Isabelle and Kate laugh in delight as he swept them along with him.

\*    \*    \*    \*    \*

# FORTUNE FAMILY TREE: THE ARIZONA BRANCH

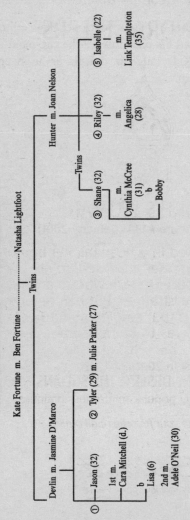

Kate Fortune m. Ben Fortune ......... Natasha Lightfoot

Twins

Hunter m. Joan Nelson

Devlin m. Jasmine D'Marco

① Jason (32)

1st m.
Cara Mitchell (d.)

b
Lisa (6)

2nd m.
Adele O'Neil (30)

② Tyler (29) m. Julie Parker (27)

Twins

③ Shane (32)
m.
Cynthia McCree (31)

b
Bobby

④ Riley (32)
m.
Angelica (28)

⑤ Isabelle (22)
m.
Link Templeton (35)

① Bride of Fortune
② Mail-Order Cinderella
③ Fortune's Secret Child
④ Husband—or Enemy?
⑤ Groom of Fortune

d.   deceased
.....   affair

If you enjoyed what you just read,
then we've got an offer you can't resist!

# Take 2 bestselling love stories FREE!

# Plus get a FREE surprise gift!

**Clip this page and mail it to Silhouette Reader Service™**

**IN U.S.A.**
3010 Walden Ave.
P.O. Box 1867
Buffalo, N.Y. 14240-1867

**IN CANADA**
P.O. Box 609
Fort Erie, Ontario
L2A 5X3

**YES!** Please send me 2 free Silhouette Desire® novels and my free surprise gift. Then send me 6 brand-new novels every month, which I will receive months before they're available in stores. In the U.S.A., bill me at the bargain price of $3.34 plus 25¢ delivery per book and applicable sales tax, if any*. In Canada, bill me at the bargain price of $3.74 plus 25¢ delivery per book and applicable taxes**. That's the complete price and a savings of at least 10% off the cover prices—what a great deal! I understand that accepting the 2 free books and gift places me under no obligation ever to buy any books. I can always return a shipment and cancel at any time. Even if I never buy another book from Silhouette, the 2 free books and gift are mine to keep forever. So why not take us up on our invitation. You'll be glad you did!

225 SEN C222
326 SEN C223

| | | |
|---|---|---|
| Name | (PLEASE PRINT) | |
| Address | Apt.# | |
| City | State/Prov. | Zip/Postal Code |

\* Terms and prices subject to change without notice. Sales tax applicable in N.Y.
\*\* Canadian residents will be charged applicable provincial taxes and GST.
   All orders subject to approval. Offer limited to one per household.
   ® are registered trademarks of Harlequin Enterprises Limited.

DES00                                    ©1998 Harlequin Enterprises Limited

# COMING NEXT MONTH

### #1339 TALL, DARK & WESTERN—Anne Marie Winston
*Man of the Month*

Widowed rancher Marty Stryker needed a wife for his young daughter, so he placed an ad in the paper. When attractive young widow Juliette Duchenay answered his ad, the chemistry between them was undeniable. Marty knew he was falling for Juliette, but could he risk his heart for a second chance at love and family?

### #1340 MILLIONAIRE M.D.—Jennifer Greene
*Texas Cattleman's Club: Lone Star Jewels*

When Winona Raye discovered a baby girl on her doorstep, wealthy surgeon Justin Webb proposed a marriage of convenience to give the child a family. But for Winona, living under the same roof with the sexy doctor proved to be a challenge. Because now that Justin had the opportunity to get close to Winona, he was determined to win her heart.

### #1341 SHEIKH'S WOMAN—Alexandra Sellers
*Sons of the Desert*

Anna Lamb woke with no memory of her newborn baby, or of the tall, dark and handsome sheikh who claimed to be her husband. Although she was irresistibly drawn to Ishaq Ahmadi, Anna couldn't understand his anger and suspicion until the sheikh revealed his identity...and his shocking reasons for claiming *her* as his woman....

### #1342 THE BARONS OF TEXAS: KIT—Fayrene Preston
*The Barons of Texas*

Kit Baron was in serious trouble. One of her ranch hands was dead, and she was the only suspect. Then criminal lawyer Des Baron—the stepcousin Kit had always secretly loved— came to her rescue. Now he was determined to prove her innocence, but could Kit prove her love for Des?

### #1343 THE EARL'S SECRET—Kathryn Jensen

When American tour guide Jennifer Murphy met the dashing young Earl Christopher Smythe in Scotland, sparks flew. Before long their relationship became a passionate affair and Jennifer fell in love with Christopher. But the sexy earl had a secret, and in order to win the man of her dreams, Jennifer would have to uncover the truth....

### #1344 A COWBOY, A BRIDE & A WEDDING VOW—Shirley Rogers

Cowboy Jake McCall never knew he was a father until Catherine St. John's son knocked on his door. In order to get to know his son, Jake convinced Catherine to stay on his ranch for the summer. Could the determined cowboy rekindle the passion between them and persuade Catherine to stay a lifetime?

CMN1200